All Over Again

Paul & Luke Conzo

***

Read 'Em and Reap
Publishing

Table of Contents

PREFACE

Preface

I t started on a trip to the New England Air Museum in upstate Connecticut, in the summer of 2019.
As Paul and Luke Conzo were traveling from Norwalk, CT to the museum, Paul began to develop an idea for a potential book. Paul, Luke's dad, asked him to find a piece of paper and something to write with.

As Paul began to recite the thoughts in his mind, thoughts regarding the book and its story, Luke reinforced some of these ideas with his thoughts. After enjoying time at the museum, Paul and Luke traveled back, continuing to come up with new ideas. The first draft was on three pieces of paper that Paul and Luke could barely decipher. Only we never knew that those three unintelligible pieces of paper would evolve into a stylistically dense, 37-chapter, 200-page-plus opus.

Luke was twelve at the time, and Paul was sixty-one. Paul has always desired to write a book, but lacks the writing skills necessary to write a book. Luke, on the other hand, has good writing skills, and likes coming up with story ideas of his own, but at the time had never thought of writing novels. Paul was never a big reader, isn't very good with his spelling abilities, and types with two fingers. However, he is very good with narration and storytelling.

Luke, however, is an exceptional reader, also has exceptional spelling and typing skills, and has the ability to write chapters and passages in different styles. But because of the age difference between Luke and Paul, Luke has limited knowledge of real life, and therefore struggles to portray certain situations or characters in realistic ways. When we started writing, we began with the overall structure of the book, and created several documents, one of which we heavily relied on, the "Chapter Plots" document. We began to write in this document, creating new chapters and formulating the storylines as they pertained to the chapters. We would write the title of the chapter, then summarize the plot of the chapter in a few bullet points.

Once this was finished, we began to create documents for each chapter. All in all, the process of completing this book took us a solid four years. This was mainly due to the both of us becoming preoccupied with responsibilities, between Luke and his schoolwork and church services (his involvement in his church's worship team, etc.), and Paul with his projects around the home, and his dedication to all the places he brought Luke to—this, as a result, delayed the book's development.

But we would never sacrifice our involvement with our church for writing this book, and it was important to us that we fulfill our responsibilities, while also continuing to write this book as a side project.

As for Denise, Paul's wife and Luke's mom, we thank her for not getting on our case when we found ourselves behind the computer for several hours, tirelessly working on this project. If anything, she probably was happy that she had some time to herself.

Also, this book would have never been possible if it were not for Paul and Luke and their ability to combine their talents as one and support each other throughout the writing process. The two of us worked very well together and heavily relied on each other in many ways.

In the process of writing this book, we had originally planned to write it in a traditional literary style. We had planned to write it like your normal novel. What followed was a series of ideas that, in turn, culminated in a series of literary styles.

We found ourselves having a lot of fun creating new literary styles for chapters. Some styles we came up with ourselves, while other styles have been commonly used by writers. While these styles can be fun to experience as you read this book, these styles can also feel abrupt and sudden at times.

While this can be challenging for some readers, it will also help you become familiar with diverse literary styles.

All in all, we had a great time writing this book, we hope you have a great time reading this book, and ultimately, we hope that you are encouraged by the message of this book. God bless you.

Paul & Luke Conzo

All Over Again

CHAPTER 1

The Morning

"What good deeds have I done?"

A Saturday morning.

"Hey, Mason! Let's go!" my wife Abigail called from the kitchen.

Mason refrained from leaving her bedroom.

"Gee, how many times are you gonna call her, Mom?" Madison asked curiously.

"Oh, well, she'll just have to deal with cold pancakes," Abigail said.

After all, Mason would take some leisurely time to herself before arriving at the kitchen table. Abigail and I deeply love Mason, but Mason just needs some guidance from us.

"Well, that's what happens when you're in a

house full of women," I exclaimed as I opened the refrigerator door to grab the orange juice.

"Hey, Dad! I'm never late," Madison zestfully responded.

"Well, maybe you were supposed to be the boy we never had," I responded. I mean, I did want to have a male child. At least, I wouldn't feel outnumbered in this family.

"So what are you, disappointed that I wasn't a boy?" Madison asked me, appearing puzzled by my remark.

"Well, sometimes, I guess I'm just better off keeping my mouth closed," I admitted.

"That is a good idea, actually," my wife chimed in amidst the argument my daughters and I were having.

Mason entered the kitchen, overhearing our argument. As Mason approached an open chair, she said, "Maybe you should only open your mouth when you're eating, Dad."

"Okay, enough with the jokes now, everyone," Abigail interrupted, grabbing her scripture notes from the kitchen counter. Abigail then brought the notes to the table for her daily morning devotional based on a scripture that she normally reads to our family.

"Now, first off, I want to start off our day with a scripture I really like," Abigail began, preparing to read aloud.

"Alright, Mom," Madison replied in agreement. Now, Abigail was ready to start reading her scripture notes.

Her notes were extensive sometimes, as she was devout in her service to the faith. She would frequently take notes on scriptures and other religious sources. I, personally, am not a devout follower, but I still believe in the faith. I still attend studies and other religious gatherings.

"Calling all ears now," Abigail announced, "I'm going to read this scripture now. It says here, '*You are the light of the world. A town built on a hill cannot be hidden. Neither do people light a lamp and put it under a bowl. Instead they put it on its stand, and it gives light to everyone in the house. In the same way, let your light shine before others, that they may see your good deeds and glorify your Father*'. I really like this scripture, because it really speaks from the heart to me."

"Yeah, well, what good deeds have I done?" I skeptically responded to her message, questioning the scripture. I could've done more good deeds.

"Come on, honey, what makes you think you're a failure, Brian?" Abigail kindly asked, consolingly patting me on the back.

"Maybe it's because I'm not a boy," Madison said.

I then realized that Madison was starting to think differently about my reason for disappointment. I wasn't disappointed because she was a female, it was because I feel regret for not making a difference. I don't think I've done enough for other people in the past, and sometimes the thought of it just haunts me.

"Now, Brian, I could name a list of contributions that you have made to this family," Abigail reminded me, "First of all, you are the main provider for this family, and second of all, you are a loving husband and father to our children. You mean a lot to us. Third of all, you are also very eager to have family gatherings. That's just a few of the many things you do for this family."

While Abigail's words were reassuring to me, I still felt as if I could've done more for other people who were in need.

"And Dad, as you know, I am very late for breakfast a lot of times, but you never get angry at me," Mason exclaimed, then turning to my wife with piercing eyes, "But with Mom, it's a different story."

"You stop right there, girl!" Abigail strictly interjected Mason's remark.

"Okay everyone, let's just listen to Mom's direction for the day, alright?" I calmly reminded everyone at the table.

It was time for my wife to start handing out responsibilities for our 25th anniversary party. Abigail was now ready to give out tasks to complete for the party.

"Alright, everybody, now listen closely," Abigail announced, "We will have to arrive at the Apple Grove church hall by noon for our 4:00 party today. We're going to set up many decorations for the party, along with finishing up the favors. We're going to assign you duties now. You, Madison, are going to be in charge of completing the favors. You, Mason, help with the decorations. I'm going to wrap up my baking, and you, Brian, you're going to bring the family to the church hall by noon. The car's already loaded with everything from last night. At around 2:00, your cousins, Samuel, Travis, and Morgan are all going to show up to offer some assistance, and you, Brian, will instruct Samuel and Travis to set up the chairs."

My two daughters responded by shaking

their heads, probably thinking to themselves of the negative effects of having Samuel and Travis over. After all, I think they could be a little bit annoying at times, so I could understand how my daughters felt about them. I'll just get Samuel and Travis to follow my instructions. As for Morgan, the girls will love spending time with her, and will perfectly get along.

Breakfast was almost over by now. Mason was still eating her pancakes, but Madison and I were already finished with our breakfast.

"Madison, it's your turn to do the dishes now," Abigail reminded Madison after she had finished her breakfast. Madison followed Abigail's directions and walked over to the counter to do the dishes. After all, Madison wasn't the kind of daughter to give Abigail a hard time, contrary to Mason, who would sometimes be resistant to Abigail's instructions. I like Madison's devotion to our family, and I think she contributes a lot.

Mason, on the other hand, will eventually listen to our directions, but usually needs some prompting before doing so. Overall, I love both of them, and they are both good girls.

6

"Alright, Mason, once you're finished with your pancakes, this table needs to be cleaned up," Abigail said, "After all, I have to finish some baking for the party."

As Abigail was gathering her baking ingredients, she realized she was out of vanilla extract. She had a surprised look on her face as she came up to me.

Abigail said, "Hey, honey, I just ran out of vanilla extract. I'm definitely going to need some. Would you be kind to go out and get some for me at the store?"

"Alright, Abigail, I'll get some for you," I promised, then kissed her on the cheek.

As I was about to leave, I heard Mason calling as she headed upstairs, "And Dad, while you're at it, could you get some Q-tips for me?"

"Okay," I responded, "And by the way, does anybody else need something before I leave?"

Madison and Abigail both confirmed that they were all set.

CHAPTER 2

The Preparation

"Wear the silver tie."

We arrived at the hall at 12:00, preparing for the anniversary party. There were many chairs on both sides of the hall, having been put away on their racks. The tables were up against the walls as well, turned on their sides. When Samuel and Travis show up at 2:00, I will get them to help out with setting up the tables and chairs.

So far, Madison was working very hard at preparing the favors, which were made up of nicely wrapped pastries, including freshly baked cookies. Madison was doing a beautiful job at tying the bows on the favors. Mason was starting to hang up ribbons and silver-colored balloons, which represent platinum for the 25th anniversary, as decorations for the party.

Meanwhile, I was helping Mason hang some ribbons, being that some of them were difficult and required a ladder to hang them up.

My wife, Abigail, made a phone call with the caterer and florist, confirming with them that the food and cake would arrive on time, along with the table flowers.

***

It was almost 2:00 now, and we were almost finished with our tasks. The only things we had left to do were setting up tables, chairs, tablecloths, and the table flowers. In only a few more minutes, Samuel and Travis would arrive here to help us out.

"Wait a second, they're here," Mason observed, upon noticing that a car had pulled up in the parking lot.

"Who's here?" Madison asked.

"Aunt Julia and Uncle Benjamin are pulling into the parking lot now," Mason said, peering through the window.

Abigail approached my two daughters, ready to inform them about something.

"By the way, girls," Abigail informed them sternly, "make sure to show some respect towards Samuel and Travis. I don't want to see you ignoring them."

Being that Samuel and Travis could be annoying sometimes, Mason and Madison would still have to be nice toward them.

A few minutes later, Samuel and Travis entered through the door, approaching me. They looked prepared for work, so that was when I informed them of what they needed to do.

Then, Samuel and Travis both walked over to the tables and chairs, and started setting them up for the party. As the tables and chairs were being set up, the girls started putting the tablecloths and flower arrangements on the tables.

Once we had finished working on the tables and other arrangements for the party, the food had arrived, having been delivered by the caterer. The caterer placed the trays of food on the food table.

I then realized that I had forgotten my tie for the party. I had to let everybody know that I needed to leave in order to get my tie.

11

As I was starting to prepare to leave, I noticed my two daughters walking to the door to greet their Aunt Olivia and their Uncle Jack, along with their cousin Morgan. The girls jubilantly greeted Morgan as they started talking with her.

Then I approached Abigail to inform her of my brief departure from the hall.

"Okay, I gotta leave for a moment, Abigail," I said, "Forgot my tie, I need to get it now."

"Alright, honey," she calmly replied, "Just make sure to wear the silver tie."

"Why the silver tie?" I questioned her remark. After all, the silver tie I had was getting a little old-fashioned, and I wasn't very fond of wearing it.

"Well, it represents platinum for our 25th anniversary," Abigail reminded me.

"Alright, I guess I'll wear it," I said, "Would you like for me to wear my silver socks as well?"

"No, that won't be necessary," Abigail said, now chuckling, "But you could wear your silver nail polish."

The two of us laughed at the joke. Abigail was always the type to sprinkle humor into a situation. I like that about her.

"Is there anything else that you would want me to get?" I asked.

"No, that'll be all," Abigail said, then leaving to direct others, including Samuel and Travis, with additional tasks, since they had already finished the tables and chairs.

I approached the exit, and saw that my two daughters and Morgan were doing fine, as they usually do. They were all talking and having fun with each other.

I then exited the hall, and, when walking to my car, looked up and saw a commercial airline which reminded me of the vacation we hadn't been able to take this year. Hopefully next year we can afford a family vacation. After all, family time is important, and Abigail has also been asking me for the past four years if we could travel on a cruise to the Caribbean. I then drove off, heading towards the house.

***

On my way back to the hall, having put on my silver tie, I pondered the speech I would be giving at the party. I'm actually pretty lucky that I arrived home to get my tie, because sitting on the kitchen table was my speech transcript.

Oh dear, had I forgotten that, I would have a loss for words, and that would be an embarrassment. It's funny how I have the ability to speak at my financial meetings with no problems, but when making a speech in front of my family and friends, I tend to have a loss for words.

Now, my wife, on the other hand, wouldn't have a problem making a speech. She could be a chatterbox at times, though.

I then arrived at the hall, seeing that more cars had pulled into the parking lot. As I was approaching the hall, I saw the production crew unloading a truck filled with sound equipment. They were bringing out some loudspeakers, as well.

I then walked towards the hall, and opened the door to find my two daughters and Morgan having fun together. I also noticed that the decorations had been completed, with help from Samuel and Travis. Frankly, I'm surprised that both boys accomplished more than I originally expected.

"Wow, what an excellent job. Everything looks great!" I said to my helpers. I was very thankful for the help I got in preparing for this special occasion.

I now had my silver tie on, and I admit, it looked pretty nice for the party. Not for long, more people should be arriving soon. I was definitely looking forward to talking with my friends and family. Some of my friends I hadn't seen in some time, and I would like to catch up with them. It's nice to see how people are doing, after all.

CHAPTER 3

The Celebration

"The floor is all yours."

"**B**rian, the guests are about to arrive," Abigail reminded me, "And don't forget to smile."

"Oh, come on, I always smile," I replied with a grin.

"Well, it didn't look that way at breakfast time this morning," Abigail said. Yeah, I suppose it didn't look that way at breakfast time.

I then informed Abigail that I would be at the entrance greeting the guests as they arrived in the church hall. I then started to make my way towards the entrance door. As I made my way there, I noticed Jane Reed coming in through the entrance, walking with someone who appeared to be different from her last boyfriend. I was actually surprised to see her come so early, being she would usually be late whenever she was invited to an event.

"Hello, Jane," I said, "Glad you could be here today. Haven't seen you in a while."

"Well, you know me," Jane responded, "Always on the go, and ready to show."

"Where's Donny?" I asked.

"Well, I recall that was about two boyfriends ago," Jane said, "I think I might've lost track. Well, meet Alfred. We've been going for just about a couple weeks now."

"Well, nice to meet you, Alfred," I said to him, then added quietly, "Hope to see you again."

I paused for a minute, directing them towards the church hall to meet Abigail, who was there to greet them.

I then turned to greet other guests as they were entering the building. As guests were coming through, I noticed George Davis entering with Derek Whitman.

Hmm. Which reminds me. George the stoner, Derek the ex-con. Wonder what schemes they got cooking.

As they were both walking together, George said, "Hey, Brian! Long time no see!"

"25 years married," Derek said, "Doesn't it feel like 25 years in the pen, Brian?"

"Well, guys," I replied, chuckling, "I'm sure we've got a lot to talk about. Head towards the church hall and Abigail will direct you to your cells—oh, please excuse me, I mean chairs."

We all laughed, and the two of them headed toward the church hall.

I continued greeting guests as they entered; this is when I noticed that some of Abigail's family had entered the building. I greeted them and then directed them to Abigail.

I then walked back to the entrance door to find Charles Harrison and his wife walking through the door.

"Hey, Charles," I said as he approached me, "Sorry to hear about the election loss. Hope that things turn out better for you next run."

"Well, that's alright, there's other elections coming up, so at least that's good," Charles responded.

"Well, if it helps, you have my vote, Charles," I said as he walked past me, "Where are the kids?"

"Oh, I left them with my first wife," Charles

said, "Do you know, this is my third?"

"And your last," Charles' wife quickly cut in.

"Well, Abigail's right through the door to greet you," I said, "Well, hope you enjoy your time."

As I continued greeting guests as they came in, I then noticed a cab pull up. The cab driver walked out of the car, and opened the door for the passenger to get out. Once the passenger got out of the car, I then noticed that the passenger was Sally Hanks, and the cab driver was Rocco Lombardi.

As Sally and Rocco both proceeded to enter the building, I was hoping Rocco was in a good mood, being his temper and all. I was thinking that I should've hired a couple bouncers for the party. Sally, on the other hand, is an easier cookie to handle than Rocco.

They both came in, Rocco first greeting me with a firm handshake, a slap on the back, and a bear hug.

"How's things going, Brian?" Rocco asked.

"Well, it's nice to see the both of you," I said, "How's the cab business been going, Rocco? And how's your singing, Sally?"

"Well, the cab business sort of keeps my head above water," Rocco said, "So at least that's good."

"As for my singing, uh..." Sally paused for a minute, "I only do my singing in the shower, and that's all."

"Well, hope you guys have a good time," I said, "You can step right this way and Abigail will meet you."

After I directed them to Abigail, I headed into the hall and joined the people who were eating the appetizers, which were lined up on a table.

Oh, there's Benjamin, Abigail's brother-in-law, hovering over the calamari. He's not gonna leave that spot, that's for sure. I'm surprised he doesn't fill his pockets. I don't know what Abigail's sister Julia saw in him. I walked over to where Benjamin was as he scanned through the appetizers. I didn't make it to the calamari in time, unfortunately, so I went for the chicken wings before he got to them. After I had some of the chicken wings, I noticed Olivia, Abigail's sister, approaching me as I stood by the appetizer table.

She informed me that Abigail said that dinner would be ready in about 20 minutes. Her husband Jack is helping out with the photography for our anniversary, which we so appreciate. I'm hoping he does a great job, being he bummed up our wedding photos.

After I talked with Olivia, I saw that my Uncle Bob, my mom's brother, was approaching me. I always used to joke around a lot about Uncle Bob; being his last name was Conroy, I'd always joke around and call him "Conman". He always had a story to tell, and I'm still trying to figure out whether I believed them or not.

"Hey, Brian! Boy, I got some stories to tell you," Uncle Bob shouted.

"Oh, well, could you keep it to one story, Uncle Bob?" I jokingly replied.

As Uncle Bob started telling the story, I noticed my Mom, Dad, and my brother Leonard. Leonard was usually late for special occasions. I think if he had a wife, she'd straighten him out.

As Uncle Bob continued his story, I then recognized that Uncle Bob was telling the same story he'd told me at least five times before, and I painfully struggled to pretend as if I'd never heard the story before. All in all, Uncle Bob is my favorite uncle.

As Uncle Bob now started to join some of the other guests, I walked over to Jeffrey, Abigail's brother, who was talking to Pamela, his wife.

"Hey, Jeffrey," I said, "How's the house hunting going?"

"Well," Pamela intervened, "it'd be going a lot better if Jeffrey would at least make the effort to hunt for the house."

"Oh, come on now," Jeffrey answered, "You know I'm working two shifts."

"Well, I'm working three shifts," Pamela said, "One to upkeep the house, one to upkeep the kids, and one to upkeep you." We all laughed at the joke, and then continued talking for a while before Abigail rang the bell for the 5-minute warning for dinner.

**

It was dinnertime now, and as quiet music played from the speakers, all the guests were directed towards their respective seats by Abigail. Once everyone had been seated, Abigail opened with the blessing.

"Father God," Abigail began, "we thank you for this night where we can gather together and celebrate this time with friends and family. We ask you to bless this night and bless this food to our bodies, in Jesus' name, Amen, and, as they say, *buon appetito a tutti*."

Abigail began to direct the guests to go up in an orderly fashion to get their food. Once everyone got their food and sat down to eat, soft and quiet music continued to play in the background.

When everyone was finished with the main course, the dance floor opened and the music started to kick up a beat; people started to approach the dance floor and danced for quite some time.

And as the night went by, and everyone was all tuckered out, dessert was almost ready, so Abigail reminded me to make my speech first before dessert would be served. Then, Abigail proceeded to approach the stage, and then got everyone's attention to inform them that I was going to make my speech. As she spoke, I recognized the song that faintly played through the speakers—my favorite song.

She then concluded her brief speech to the crowd with, "The floor is all yours," and that's when I hit the floor.

CHAPTER 4

The Awakening

"How did I get here?"

"Brian!!!"
My mother was calling me, but her voice sounded like that of the past. As I opened my eyes in a room that was coated with shades of dark, light shades of dark—my eyes were in a bit of a blurred state, I suppose, but I managed to keep them open, despite the blurred state they were in—it all still felt a little foggy, but eventually things started to get into focus, and that's when I began to pick up my surroundings more, and I started to process

where I was. The room looked quite like that of my younger days, and I was especially surprised yet simultaneously troubled by this. It all felt a bit like an anomaly, an oddity, an irregularity that all felt so strange, so bizarre.

As I sat up in bed, I noticed my reflection in the mirror across the room—a reflection of myself, only it was a different self, a different person, a different me—yes, it was indeed me, but it was—yes, perhaps it was a different version of me.

That's when my mind starts to whirl back and forth and back and forth and back and forth, and it continues in the utter confusion that I now found myself in—yes, it was complete confusion—I see a younger me, a younger self—perhaps it is a younger self with an existing mind as I was—yes, this was my younger self, and it was then that I came to the conclusion that if this were to be my younger self, then it was to be—

"Brian! You'll be late for school!"

It was my mother again. That was when I realized that I had better get dressed, go downstairs, and then perhaps I'd see what I was truly in for; as I was rounding the corner at the bottom of the staircase, looking into the kitchen, I saw my breakfast on the table, and the back of my mother, who was at the sink.

As bizarre as this was, I supposed it was best that I go along with the surreal nightmare of it all. I walked over to the table, stood there for a couple seconds, and my mother then turned toward me, looking at me strangely.

"What are you just standing there for?" my mother said, appearing concerned, "Aren't you going to eat? You'll be late."

"Alright, Mom," I responded hesitantly.

"Are you okay today, Brian?" she asked, still troubled.

"Oh, yes, I'm fine," I nervously said, "I'll be better after I eat, though."

I sat down to eat my breakfast, which was my mother's signature pancakes, which she was famously known for by relatives and friends. As I smelled the sweet aroma emanating from the pancakes, my younger brother walked in and sat down to eat his pancakes.

My brother and I talked for a while, before I had realized that it was time to go. I quickly rushed, then saying goodbye to my brother and mother—my father was already out to work—I then opened the door leading outside, and left, still puzzled at the surreal nightmare that I was still experiencing.

***

As I approached my bicycle, I realized that I hadn't ridden a bike in quite some time. For some strange reason, I hopped on the bike and went on my way effortlessly. I met with my friend Harry Ferguson and we went off to school on our bikes.

As we rode on our bikes, I continued thinking about what was happening to me. How did I get here? What brought me here? What kind of strange occurrence or situation brought me to this moment?

Was this real? As a matter of fact, was any of it real? Perhaps it could have just been a dream, a trance, a reverie—yes, perhaps it was that—perhaps it was a simple daydream.

At least, that's what I hoped it was.

CHAPTER 5

The Opportunity

"Sounds like an interesting place."

A s we were riding our bikes to school, I was hitting Harry with a lot of questions. It looked like Harry was getting tired of it, actually. For a second he looked at me like I was crazy or something.

***

"Hey, uh, Harry."
"Yes."
"What class do we have first today?"
"Oh, well, you should know that one.

You know Mr. Rogers, don't you?"
"Oh, I remember now."
I don't know what's gotten into Brian today.
He's acting a bit strange. It's not normal. He
never acts like this. At least, I've never seen
him act this way. Asking me all these crazy
questions about things he should already
know. It just feels strange for him to do this
today. I guess it's because it's the morning
and all—it's the morning that can do things
to you sometimes—but nonetheless, it all
feels strange anyway. Sounds like he's
another person in his body. But I don't know.
Who knows?

***

As I left school for the day and headed
towards my bike, I felt eerie, anomalous
feelings as they began to dawn over me. I
couldn't remember some people's names,
but I suppose it's normal, being I haven't
been in this body for over 30 years. That
explains why I was messing up today. I don't
know if I could get used to this. It's so
strange, the feeling of being trapped in one's
younger body. God, please let this be a
dream. I hope it is. At least, I'd like to hope
so.

As I was riding my bike through the town of Apple Grove, I came upon a jiu-jitsu place, instantly recalling to mind what Harry had told me as we were riding our bikes to school this morning. Harry was telling me about how his dad wanted him to get involved in jiu-jitsu, so I naturally asked about the sport and what it was all about. He then started telling me more about how jiu-jitsu involves martial arts and self-defense, except jiu-jitsu is a more—yes, tame, I suppose—version of self-defense. It doesn't involve any of the punching and kicking that's commonly attributed to other forms of self-defense— rather, it involves the "grappling" style of martial arts.

I then decided to stop in and see what it was all about. Since I've thought about being involved in a sport, why not have it be jiu-jitsu?

I looked at some of the brochures they had at the place. Then I brought some of them home and showed them to my dad. If anything comes out of this, it'll keep my mind off of the craziness and confusion I've been experiencing today. It was then time that I head off to bed, so I changed into my pajamas, brushed my teeth, and headed back into my bedroom, shutting the lights out, hoping this is all a dream. Time for bed now. I suppose it's best that I get some sleep. Oh, boy. I didn't realize how uncomfortable this bed actually was. Man, this is actually very uncomfortable, now that I think about it.

CHAPTER 6

The Road Trip

"I've got a premonition."

Boy, this bed's not only uncomfortable, it's also kind of bumpy, too. Oh dear. I suppose it's time to get up now.

To my surprise, I found myself in the backseat of my dad's old Chevrolet, with my younger brother Leonard, who was sound asleep. We were traveling down the interstate.

The last thing I remembered was that I was home in bed. It all felt very strange. I'm in bed one minute, and the next minute I find myself in the back of my dad's Chevrolet.

I hope this ends soon. I really hope it does. All this confusion.

"Where am I now?" I asked my mom and dad, begging for an answer, "Who did this? Who put me here?"

"Are you crazy, Brian?" my father turned around and looked over at me in puzzlement, "We just left our house an hour ago. You don't remember that?"

"To travel where?" I asked.

"To travel to the place you've wanted to go to all winter long. You know, Beaver Lake Park?"

"Oh, okay, I understand now."

I lay back against my seat, now finally somewhat relaxed. As I lay back against the seat, in what at first seemed to be a moment of undisturbed relaxation, a memory started to enter my mind.

It was a memory of my father. And the event happened in this car. Yes, it was when my father drove to a gas station, got into a Fender Bender as he was driving there, and lost his pocket watch. It was a terrible day for my father, being that his losing the pocket watch was more important to him than the dent that would be planted in the side of his car.

"Well, I suppose we ought to stop at a gas

station now," my father suggested, "Could stop at the gas station coming up ahead." There was silence in the car for several seconds. I thought about what I would say to my dad, something, anything to prevent him from losing that darned pocket watch. It was a precious gem, that pocket watch. It was inherited from his grandfather, and it was worth quite some money. I don't even think he slept for two months after losing that watch. Yes, it was quite a precious gem to him.

It was time for me to come up with something to say right now. Yes, it was time now.

"Hey, Dad," I began in a faltering voice.

"Yes, son?" He turned to face me for a moment, then refocused his eyes on the road.

"I don't think you should go to that gas station, Dad."

"And why is that?"

"I've got a premonition," I said, now contented and regaining confidence.

"What kind of premonition you got?" he said, lightly chuckling.

"I've got a feeling there's another gas station up ahead."

"What gas station? Why can't we just go to

the one down on the left?"

"Well, if you're looking for more expensive gas, then by all means, choose it."

I mean, I had to come up with some sort of a convincing excuse. Anything to avoid the disaster that would ensue.

"How can you possibly know this gas is too expensive?" my dad asked, still puzzled.

"As I said earlier, I have a premonition."

"I didn't know you knew that word 'premonition' at such a young age."

"Well, let's just say that lately, I've been feeling like I have an adult mind in a child's body."

After all, it was true. Of course, it came off as a joke at the moment, but I'm not experiencing this joke too well.

As we were pulling up to the gas station several miles down the road, we came to find that the gas was ten cents more a gallon.

"Oh, you and your premonition," my dad said as he pulled into the gas station, "This is coming out of your allowance, I just want you to know that."

"Well, it's better than a Fender Bender and a missing pocket watch," I mumbled under my breath.

Well, I guess I saved my father two months of sleepless and insomnia-riddled nights.

CHAPTER 7

The Dinner

"Home at last."

*T*he Marinos have arrived home, the car *is still in one piece, and the pocket watch is still ticking. The Marinos have now entered the house, carrying their luggage and souvenirs.*

The father, MARK, hangs up his coat, still nagging BRIAN about the gas station situation. BRIAN then follows after MARK and hangs up his coat. MARK leaves, and BRIAN follows.

Meanwhile, BRIAN's mother, LINDA, starts dinner, and BRIAN's brother, LEONARD, walks about aimlessly for a couple seconds before going upstairs to unpack his luggage.

LINDA
(calling out)
Just so you all know, tonight is whip-it-up night for dinner! Everything should be ready in about thirty minutes or so.

MARK
(enters the kitchen)
I'm sure it'll be fine, dear. Anything you make is always good. [pauses for a second as he opens the refrigerator] Well, here we are. Home at last. [pauses] What are we having for dinner, anyway?

LINDA
Well, I was planning on making those two frozen pizzas in the freezer.

MARK
Yeah, I suppose we could.

MARK, after looking around the refrigerator for several seconds, closes it, and walks about the kitchen.

LINDA
You know, it was pretty nice out there at Beaver Lake Park, wasn't it?

MARK
Yeah, it was pretty nice, but maybe next year, we can do something different.

LINDA
(in a curious voice)
Like what?

MARK
I was thinking we camp out in the mountains.

LINDA
The mountains? I was thinking we could go to the shore.

BRIAN and LEONARD, overhearing the conversation, run into the kitchen.

LEONARD
(ecstatic)
Maybe we could go to the amusement park.

BRIAN
Yeah, the mountains are too dangerous, you
know, 'cause they have bears and poison ivy. I
just don't think it's safe. The shore's dangerous
as well. There's sharks! And as for the
amusement park, the rides could be dangerous.

BRIAN
[cont'd]
How about if we go to a museum? That might be
safer.

LINDA
(puzzled)
What are you so worried about this "safety"
thing for?

BRIAN
Well, I guess I've got another premonition.

MARK
(in a louder voice)
Oh, you and your premonitions! How about if
we go skiing or sky-diving? You got an issue

with that?

LINDA
(in a calmer tone)
Okay, we'll be having dinner soon. Let's settle down.

The Marinos have now settled down. Dinner will be ready soon, and all is at rest in the Marino household.

***

The Marinos are now having dinner, and as usual, they have a lot to say at dinnertime. LEONARD grabs the ketchup and squirts some on his pizza. He then spreads the ketchup on the pizza with his fork.

BRIAN
So now you know why me and Leonard don't get along? Anyone who puts ketchup on his pizza has got to have some internal issues.

LINDA
(in a serious tone)
Come on now, Brian. Do you remember the time when you put pickles on your ice cream?

41

BRIAN
(shrugs)
Well, that was four years ago when I was eight.

LINDA
(reminding BRIAN)
Well, Leonard's only ten.

MARK
Well, we ought to go to bed early tonight. I gotta go to work tomorrow, so that's gonna be a bit of a rough day.

LINDA
Yes, I suppose we probably should get going to bed soon. I have laundry to do tomorrow, and I also got some grocery shopping to do.

***

The Marinos are now resting peacefully and undisturbed, after a long and restless day. And BRIAN is still thinking about the surreal nightmare of it all.

CHAPTER 8

The Poster

"TALENT SHOW THIS FRIDAY."

"**B**rian, can you snap out of it, please? We don't want daydreamers in this class." After a good night's sleep, I found myself daydreaming in my seventh-grade literature class with Mr. Dobson, who was teaching the book *The Call of the Wild*.

"So, Brian, why don't you tell the class all that you've learned about *The Call of the Wild*, being you're so attentive in this class?" Thank God I read the book recently in my adult body, so Mr. Dobson's in for a surprise. "Well, you see, *The Call of the Wild* is about a lot of things," I began, "On the one hand, it's a simple adventure story about a dog named Buck, who is stolen from his home during the 1890s Klondike Gold Rush, when strong sled dogs were in high demand. When Buck is sold as a sled dog, he gradually learns to adapt to the harsh conditions of the environment around him, where he is forced to fight to survive. By the end, he relies on his instinct and perseverance to finally emerge as a true leader of the wild.

"However, on the other hand, it's an allegory about the virtues of humanity and how humanity can succeed and triumph against even the toughest and most difficult environments and situations. On another hand, it could be a story of—

"Alright, alright, you've made your point," Mr. Dobson respectfully interrupted, "We'll talk about the themes of the book next class, since some of the students are still reading it."

The bell rang, and my best friend Harry and I got up from our chairs, quickly grabbed our books, and headed to our next class, leaving Mr. Dobson's room.

As Harry and I were walking out of Mr.

Dobson's room, Harry said, "You sounded like a scholar in there, Brian. What happened?"

"Well, I suppose it was my other personality that came out," I said to Harry, who nevertheless appeared bemused, judging by the look on his face. That was when right in front of us appeared a poster, which we both stopped to look at. The poster read:

ANNOUNCEMENT

TALENT SHOW THIS FRIDAY, 6:00PM, AUDITORIUM

COME FOR MUSIC, DANCING, FOOD, AND FUN

FREE ADMISSION TO ALL STUDENTS

After reading the poster, we decided, upon momentarily deliberating, to attend the talent show. It looked really interesting to us, especially since we hadn't been to a lot of these school events lately, with schoolwork and all. I suppose it was best for us to go to this one.

That's when a couple friends came over and saw the poster, too. They seemed pretty interested as well.

They decided to come to the talent show with us, especially when they saw the "free admission" part, and also when they saw that they were getting food.

I then wrote down the time, just to remind myself.

***

As the days went by, and Friday is just a day away, I began to notice something that felt a bit strange and off-putting to me. I was in the same place, the same realm, this week. It's hard to explain. Everything felt the same, yes, that was it, everything felt the same about the beginning of every day; every day began the same way, ended the same way, and this was all as it was approaching Friday.

It felt like life had finally reached its normality, but yet, there still felt as if there was an abnormality, an irregularity, something odd that was going on in my mind that I couldn't exactly blot out. It was a memory, yes, it was a memory of my older self that is still haunting me—yes, it still haunts me now—this memory, and now being trapped in my younger self, and that's what I felt, in a strange way—this idea of me being trapped, and I felt entrapped in my predicament, the predicament which I could not escape, and it all felt like an inescapable dream, an inescapable situation, and it all just surrounded me, this dream.

Well, I suppose I must wait and see what tomorrow will bring.

CHAPTER 9

The Talent Show

"Get out of here!"

A memory, memory of my younger self, inescapable memory, the inescapable memory, yes, the memory which one cannot escape from, despite the peace which I nonetheless find myself in now, there is still the memory, yes, that memory of my older self, in contrast to that of my younger self, my younger self which I now find myself entrapped in. An image, image of fainting, someone fainting, a bit of a blur, yes, everything appears a little blurry, out of focus, I can't see who's fainting, it's all out of focus, I see, now the image becomes a bit clearer, is that me, maybe it is me, yes, maybe so, yes, that is me, that is me fainting, is that, is, is that the party, yes, that's the anniversary, that was the anniversary of, yes, that was the 25th anniversary of me and my wife's marriage, yes, that's my wife over there, looks like her mouth is yelling out some indistinguishable words, is she saying "Brian", yes, perhaps she is, yes, I faintly hear her yelling "Brian", she stops yelling, is that me on the floor, yes, that's me on the floor, that's me laying there, isn't it, yes, that is me, is this a dream, maybe it is, perhaps it is all just a, yes, I think it is a—

"Brian, wake up!"

I now found myself awakened by my mother. A terrible dream that was, but one I certainly could not prevent from occurring. Yes, that was a terrible dream, indeed, one I should just forget about now.

That was me fainting, wasn't it? Yes, that was me fainting, and that was my wife I saw, too, yelling some indistinguishable words— yes, she was yelling "Brian"—yes, I remember it all.

It's 7:05am now. I'd better get ready and head to school.

"And Brian," my mother said, "isn't tonight

the night of the talent show?"
"Yeah, the Friday night talent show," I
replied, "I won't be eating here at home,
being they have food there."

***

It was 4:35pm. Soon I'll be at the school for
the talent show. Harry and his dad were
coming by to pick me up, since my parents
made arrangements to meet with their
insurance person.
My father insisted that I wear a belt, so I
went along with it. After I put on my belt, I
then proceeded to go downstairs and wait
for Harry and his father to come pick me up.

***

We had arrived at the school, and it was
4:51pm when I looked at the clock tower
that was down the street from the school.
Harry's dad was part of the event, and we
met with our friends, found good seats in
the front row, and waited until the talent
show began at 6:00pm. As we were waiting,
one of my friends, Corey, had a pea shooter
and thought of shooting spitballs at the kids.
Of course, knowing Corey, he would never

do this, being he was a nice kid, but there were times when he certainly felt like it. Corey always kept his opinions to himself, though.

Meanwhile, Harry was focusing a bit too much on the food.

"They got hot dogs here?" Harry asked.

"Yeah, they got hot dogs here," I responded.

"They got mustard?" he asked.

"Of course they got mustard," I said.

"They got sauerkraut?"

"Of course they got sauerkraut. They got everything you want. Come on, why are you always talking about food, Harry?"

"Yeah, you're always talking about food, Harry," Corey added to the conversation,

"Well, I suppose I could go for a hot dog myself. But then again, I gotta wash down the liverwurst my mom made for lunch today."

Liverwurst. Oh, my.

Well, anyway, the talent show started a couple minutes later. The first act was pretty good. The second act, on the other hand, was performed by Jim McDowell, so, of course, Corey probably thought—well, I thought the same—that it was indeed worthy of some spitballs. I probably shouldn't get into that one, though.

As the acts went on, they seemed to have gotten better, but every now and then, you had a blowout. I suppose blowouts do happen. Not to be rude or anything, it's just that I wasn't a big fan of some of them, to be honest.

Towards the halfway point of the show, Sally Hanks, a good friend of mine, did a ballet performance of "The Blue Danube". At the end of her performance, well, she took a bit of a tumble that, I have to admit, was pretty funny. I'd hate to say that, but it was pretty funny.

I didn't laugh, but of course, the entire audience couldn't contain themselves, most of them laughing out loud, some laughing internally.

"Get out of here!" one of them yelled out at Sally, who looked like she was getting a little teary-eyed. I honestly felt bad for her.

That was when the announcer came out and informed everyone that there was an intermission and that there would now be a food break.

CHAPTER 10

The Inspiration

"But I can easily fix that..."

B rian's friends quickly went up to the food table, and made sure that they were one of the first in line. "Those hot dogs look pretty good, don't they?" Harry said to his other two friends.

"Yeah, and they got the sauerkraut, too," Corey responded, "Maybe I'll just start off with dessert first."

"Well, I always knew you were crazy, Corey," Kevin said, "By the way, where's Brian?"

"I don't know," Corey said, "Last time I saw him, he was sitting with us."

"Well," Harry responded, "he's sure missing

out. Maybe I'll get an extra hot dog for him."
"Yeah, well, knowing you're hungry and all that, you'll probably eat it before you give it to him," Corey said as he grabbed one of the food trays.

***

As the people were heading towards the food, Brian started to exit the auditorium and proceeded to go backstage, where Sally would be.

As Brian entered backstage, he noticed Sally sitting on a chair, with her head lowered and a handkerchief in her hand. Brian approached Sally, who looked up at him, her eyes still teary and wet.

"Well, I guess you saw the catastrophe that happened up there," Sally said, "What brings you back here?"

"Well, overall, you did a relatively good job," Brian said sympathetically, "and it wasn't right how the people responded to a mishap in your performance. How long have you been dancing for?"

"Actually, this is my first time," Sally said despondently, now lowering her head in quiet despair.

"But for your first time, you did really well," Brian assuringly said.

"Actually, I'm better at singing," Sally looked back up at Brian, her eyes now dried and her expression rejuvenated.

"Did you ever think of singing?" Brian asked.

"Oh, no, I could never sing in front of everyone," Sally responded, "It took a lot for me to just dance. And I didn't even sign up to sing. I signed up to dance."

"But I can easily fix that," Brian said, "'cause I could talk to the coordinator in charge of this whole show, and they could add you in for a singing routine."

"But isn't it too late?" Sally asked.

"Well, let's just say I have some connections," Brian said.

"Well, I'm a little anxious when it comes to singing," Sally said nervously.

"All you need to do is just focus on the song and eliminate all distractions," Brian said, "Maybe you could focus on something else, like the clock in the back, and not the people. You could do it, believe me."

"I guess so," Sally replied, "I mean, I do really like singing, but they'll just laugh at me again."

"No, you could give yourself a second chance and redeem yourself," Brian said.

"Alright. I'll do it," Sally said in a now confident voice.

"You got this, alright," Brian assured her, "Well, I'll be going now. I'm looking forward to your performance, alright?"

"Okay," Sally said optimistically. Brian then started to walk off to talk to Harry's father, the coordinator of the event.

***

After talking to Harry's father, Brian proceeded to sit back down with his friends, who were sitting in their seats, waiting for the intermission to end. That was when Brian was interrogated for a relatively brief amount of time by his friends, who continued to bombard him with questions.

"Where were you?"

"Did you get any food?"

"We couldn't find you anywhere?"

"You just disappeared!"

"Harry, did you save that hot dog for Brian?"

"Well, I did for a while."

"You mean, you ate it?"

"Well, what did you want? I didn't want to let it get cold."

"Oh, that's okay," Brian said calmly, "I wasn't very hungry, anyway, so that's alright."

Meanwhile, Brian was truly thinking about getting that hot dog. Nonetheless, he concealed the thought, putting it to rest in the far corners of his mind.

The intermission had now ended, the people were heading towards their chairs, some of them already in their chairs, and the announcer had come out to announce the next acts, none of which included Sally's performance, for Sally was to be the last performer of the night.

The acts went on, many of which weren't particularly interesting, except for Molly Green's piano performance, and the night ended with Sally's return to the stage.

Her return to the stage surprised many people, with some still laughing. As the music started, Sally started to sing. It was a country song that she wrote herself; it was quite a great performance, and the people were in awe and wonder.

At the end of her performance, she received a standing ovation from the crowd, who continued to clap for her for some time before the applause died down and the curtains closed. Sally was filled with the tears of joy that flowed from her eyes, amazed at the wondrous sight that was occurring before her—all the people—yes, all those people, who had once chuckled and laughed at her mishap, now standing up to cheer her on and applaud her performance, and this was reassuring to Sally. This was her moment, and it had been her first moment in which she truly felt she succeeded, yes, she had accomplished something.

And there was Brian, standing, watching and observing all that was happening before him, remembering the outcome of Sally's performance on that fateful night when she fell and no one did anything about it, not even Brian, who sat in his seat as it happened and laughed along with the others; now it was Brian who was no longer laughing, and had instead felt pity on Sally at that moment when she fell; and it was now that Brian walked away from this event, hoping that he had made a difference.

CHAPTER 11

The Neighbor

"It's hard to let go..."

I woke up on the day of my 13th birthday, a Saturday morning, several months after the talent show. This all still feels strange to me, but I've been getting used to it now. I knew my parents were going to ask me to cut the lawn and do some chores around the house today. I guess despite the fact it's my birthday today, I'm still not exempt from my household duties. I lifted the covers off, got dressed for work, and headed downstairs for a hearty breakfast.

"Happy birthday, Brian," my family greeted me when I entered the kitchen.

"We made something special for you today," my mother said, "How's blueberry pancakes sound?"

"Sounds great," I said as I sat down at the table, "They're my favorite."

"So Brian," my father said as he sat across from me, "Looking forward to tonight's bowling and pizza?"

"I sure am, Dad," I responded as I started pouring the hot maple syrup on my pancakes.

"Do you know you're still not exempt from your chores today?" my father reminded me.

"Hey, Dad," my brother Leonard chimed in, "When do I get to do chores?"

"Well," I began, "when you're twelve, that's when they begin."

"So that's a year and ten months," my mother said as she approached the table to sit down, "and you'd better mark it on the calendar, 'cause I'm already making my lists."

"And that means you'd better enjoy the time you have," I jokingly suggested to Leonard, then chuckling after I said it.

We all ate breakfast and when it was over, my father suggested that, being it was my birthday, he would wash the dishes.

"Well, thanks, Dad," I said, "How about if I wash the dishes and you cut the lawn?"

"Hey there, kid, do you want to have a birthday party tonight?" my father said warningly.

"Oh, Dad, you know I'm just joking," I said, "Well, I ought to get the lawn mower going now."

I then approached the door, headed out, started the lawn mower, and proceeded to cut the lawn.

***

As I cut the lawn, I thought of the other people whose lawns I needed to cut. Who were they? If I remember correctly, I believe they were—yes, the first one was Mrs. Brooks. Who was the second? Yes, oh, yes, I remember now, it was Mr. Rogers. And then the third one was…I believe it was Mr. Johnson. Yes, it was Mr. Johnson.

Thank God they all lived on my block.

***

After I cut Mrs. Brooks' lawn, she reminded me that I had to do the trimming, which I did. Then I cut Mr. Rogers' lawn, and after I did that, I knocked on Mr. Johnson's door. "Good day, Mr. Johnson," I said as he opened the door slowly and came out, "Is there anything you need other than me cutting the lawn?"

It was a year and a half since Mr. Johnson's wife passed, and he still seemed to have never gotten over it. We'd hardly see him around, and he kept to himself more than he used to ever since her passing. I remember when he walked around the neighborhood, always with a smile on his face, and didn't stay in the house as often as he does now.

"Hey, Brian," Mr. Johnson said despairingly, "Do I owe you anything?"

"Oh, no, Mr. Johnson," I said, "It's still not the end of the month yet. I was just wondering if there's anything extra you needed."

"Well, you make your own judgment in what you think needs to be done around here," he responded.

"Okay, Mr. Johnson," I said, "Well, I'll get started now, okay?"

"Alright, Brian," he said, "See you next week."

Mr. Johnson turned and went back into the

house, closing the door. As I walked off, something hit me, an uncontrollable surge of sympathy and sadness, and it all just hit me at that moment, and that was when I knew, yes, that is when I knew, that I had to talk to Mr. Johnson again, that I had to confront him on this, this whole matter with his wife's passing and all, and what he's putting himself through now, and I knew that I had to say something now, yes, this was my time.

Knock-knock. Another *knock-knock*. Mr. Johnson answered the door.

"What is it, Brian?" Mr. Johnson asked.

"Well, uh," I paused, "well, you see, Mr. Johnson, I...I-I feel I need to tell you this."

"Well, what is it, Brian?" Mr. Johnson asked.

"You know," I began, "I can't imagine what you've been going through with your wife's passing, but I think that it's time that you move on and find some friends and do some fun things. You have a whole life ahead of you, and I know that your wife wouldn't want you carrying this sadness for the rest of your life.

"If something were to happen to you," I continued, "and your wife was alive, would you want her to carry the sadness for the rest of her life? I hope you're not mad at me

65

for saying this, Mr. Johnson, but I miss seeing you walking by our house, and stopping by to say 'hello'."

"Well, it's hard to let go, Brian," Mr. Johnson said, "I've been with her since grammar school, and I'm not mad at you, Brian. Thank you, Brian."

Mr. Johnson turned and went back into the house, after giving me a sincere smile.

It's strange that this is something that I would've never said without my adult self being in me. I just wish I was more bold when I was a kid—or should I say, am a kid, 'cause that's how things are turning out right now.

CHAPTER 12

The Gathering

"Well, you're a teen at last."

"Pass the pepperoni."
"I'll take a plain."
"I'll have the same. Just plain."
"This pizza sure tastes good."
"Wash your hands before you eat," my mother interrupted our eating, "You know, those bowling balls are pretty dirty."
It was the night of my 13th birthday, and we were at the bowling alley, eating some pizza for dinner and playing a couple rounds of bowling. We had finished our first round, and we would play another one after we finished eating. Then we'd finish the night

off with an ice cream cake and some cookies my mother baked.

Oh, and there's my cousin Angela. Late as usual.

After I had washed my hands, I grabbed a slice of pepperoni pizza and put it on my plate. I then walked over to where my friend Corey was sitting and sat next to him.

As we both started eating, I overheard Roy's mother talking to the other parents as they were eating.

"Yeah, Roy's a very quiet kid," Roy's mother said, "I'm surprised he even wanted to come here."

"Well, he probably just needs some help with socializing," George's father replied, "Maybe he ought to relax and have a Miller once in a while. I'll take another, please."

George's father looked to be a bit of a boozer. I could see that.

As Corey and I continued eating, we talked for several minutes about school and other situations. As we continued talking, I noticed that Rocco Lombardi and Derek Whitman were in the line next to us. Rocco's a bit of a bully, and Derek, well, knowing him, he's a bit of a drifter. As usual, they were making a ruckus in the next lane. Meanwhile, Corey and I talked a bit more until Kevin came along to join us.

"You ready to play another round?" Kevin suggested. We had finished eating by then, so we were ready to play another round.

***

We played for quite some time, and it was a pretty fun night, all in all. At least it helped me forget about the surreal dream I believed I was having. Yes, this probably was all just a dream, but at least tonight helped me forget it all. Looks like I'm up now.

"It's…it's a split!" I said to the other kids.

"A Golden Gate split!" George's father said.

"What's that one?" I asked.

"It's when the 4, 6, 7, and 10 pins are the only pins left standing," he said with a light chuckle, "That's a hard one."

"I don't know if I could do it then," I responded.

"Well, you're a teen at last," my father chimed in, "Show us what you got."

"I suppose so," I said, chuckling, as I lifted a bowling ball off the return.

As I steadily threw the ball down the lane, it turns out that it went right down the middle, between the pins.

"Well, Dad," I looked back at my father, "I guess I ain't got it."

"That's alright," my father said, "There's still a lot of game left to play."

The game went on from there, and we continued to play with vigor and spirit. As we played, I was temporarily distracted by my mother, as she brought in the cookies and ice cream cake. After briefly talking with my mother, I heard cheers.

"Hey, Harry," I said as he approached me, "How did you do?"

"Tried for a strike," Harry responded, "ended up getting a spare. It was a close one, though. Real close."

"Yeah, I always struggle on getting the strikes, too," I said.

"Yeah, those are always hard to get," Harry responded in agreement, "I wish they weren't as difficult as they are."

"It's alright, though," I said, "Spares are pretty good, too."

"Yeah, they're alright, I guess," Harry replied as we joined the others.

Roy Harold was next to us, so I asked him how he was doing. Roy and I talked a little bit, but being he's very quiet and always keeps to himself, we didn't talk much.

Roy was always like that, anyway.

On the other hand, some of the other kids that were bowling were more outgoing. Jane Reed, for instance, was quite the outgoing type. She would always say hello to me ecstatically. She was like that with everybody.

George Davis and Charles Harrison were both pretty outgoing, too. Meanwhile, Sally Hanks—well, she kind of kept to herself. Only had a few friends.

"Hey, Brian, it's your turn," George said.

"Oh, alright," I responded as I walked over to the return, where he was.

I decided to take one of the heavier bowling balls, and walked over to the bowling lane. I focused my eyes on the lane's floor for a couple seconds, before rolling the ball on the floor.

"Let's see how this one turns out," I said quietly to myself, hoping I would at least get a spare.

"It's…it's a strike!"

The other kids cheered in celebration, and I raised my fist in a moment of victory. I then lowered my fist, walking back to my seat. We then played for a little more, finished our second round of bowling, and then the ice cream cake was ready. Everyone sang

"Happy Birthday" and the rest of the night went really well.

That was one of the best nights I've had in a while, probably because of the fact that it gave me an escape, yes, an escape that I needed, anything to escape from this surreal dream I was living.

Well, I was getting used to living this dream, anyway, so it didn't matter much to me now.

CHAPTER 13

The School Dance

"It was a night to remember."

I found myself at the school dance, sleeping in a chair, next to my best friend Harry.

"Brian, wake up!" Harry said, nudging me with his elbow. I awoke from my sleep, and Harry nudged me again.

"Hey, Brian," Harry said, "There's Jennifer Rizzo. You think I should ask her to dance? How about if you ask her?"

"Well," I paused, "Excuse me, I gotta use the restroom for a second."

It was then that I realized that something

would happen in the next few minutes.

***

Is it too late? The fire alarm. Is it too late? The people were in the middle of dancing, the live band was in the middle of playing "Shout", and the place was packed with students and staff, when the alarm went off, and it all went haywire from there.
The staff and security that were at the event had been directing the frantic, panicked students through the exit doors, many students running and wandering about aimlessly, looking and searching for the exit doors; people, people, and more people kept hurrying and pushing towards the exit doors, causing a wave of panic and hysteria to spread through the crowd. Some people fell, some people were trampled on by others, some were injured in the melee that ensued, and the people who managed to make it through the exit doors entered a downpour of rain.
The fire trucks and the emergency vehicles arrived, and there we were, all of us, standing in the rain, waiting for something to hope for, something that would put an

end to this terrible night.

It was then that we found out that it was all a false alarm. Somebody pulled the fire alarm; meanwhile, some people had already left for home, and a few were carted off to the emergency room for their injuries.

It was a night to remember.

***

It's not too late. There's still time, I still have time. I remember. It was Billy Jones. Yes, it was Billy who pulled the fire alarm. And he pulled it in the hall leading toward the restroom. I believe I have time to stop this. I must stop this from happening. There's still time. Yes, there's still time.

There he is. He's heading towards the alarm. I must get there before him.

I then proceeded to lean up against the wall, next to the fire alarm.

"So, Brian," Billy approached me, "What are you doing leaning up against the wall?"

"Well, I'd hate to see this fire alarm go off," I said, "It'd be terrible if everyone ran out in the rain, maybe even got hurt."

"But what makes you think somebody's gonna pull it?" Billy asked, visibly confused.

"Well, it's just a premonition," I responded to Billy, who turned and walked away.

"Hey, Billy," I called out, "There's another fire alarm on the other side of the building. You wanna make sure nobody pulls that one?"

Billy turned his head, glanced back at me, and gave me a wave with his hand, as if to say, "yeah, whatever".

As I headed back towards my seat, I saw Harry, still sitting in his seat, watching the dance.

"Harry," I asked, "How'd it go with Jennifer? Did you ask her to dance?"

"Well," Harry said, "I got up to ask her, but as I started to approach her, Johnny Parsons, you know, the football star—he went up to her and asked her two seconds before I had a chance to approach her. Of course, her eyes lit up for him, so I don't have a chance there."

"Come on, Harry," I said, "You're always encouraging me. You ought to go back over there again and ask her."

"Never mind, Brian," Harry shrugged.

We continued to watch the dance for a little while before we got up and decided to leave. After all, school dances can be boring, especially when you can't dance.

As we walked out, the rain stopped, thankfully. We continued to walk along and talk for a little bit. I was going to share with Harry what was going on, but, knowing he would find it hard to believe, I decided to drop the subject and keep it to myself.

"You know, when I'm eighteen," Harry said as we walked along, "I'm thinking of having a career in the military."

"What are you thinking, Harry?" I asked, "Army, Navy, Air Force, Marines?"

"I don't know, Brian," he said quietly, "Maybe the Navy. I've never been on a boat before."

"Well," I said, "I think the Navy would be good for you."

"You think so?" Harry asked, looking up at me.

"The Navy seems to be the safest of them all, from what I've heard," I replied.

"I guess Navy it is," Harry said, "How about you, Brian? What do you want to be?"

"Well, I got a feeling I'm gonna go into finance," I said, "I already know a lot about it, you know, stocks and bonds, insurance, investing, that kind of thing."

"Well, how do you know these things?" Harry questioned me, wearing an inquiring look across his face.

"Yeah, I guess, the best way I could explain it

is that," I paused reflectively, "I feel I have an adult mind in a kid's body. Have you ever felt that way?"

"No, but I'd like to," Harry said with a laugh. We continued to talk as we walked along on the dark and moonless night.

CHAPTER 14

The Witness

"Hey, kid, where you going?"

Spring recess was over, and I woke up on a school day. I don't even know what grade I'm in, or how old I am. Probably around 14, but I don't know. Who knows? I'll have to look at the calendar. My mother made a nice breakfast for my brother and I today. Those egg omelets she makes are pretty good.

"Don't want to be late for school, Brian," my mother reminded me when I was almost finished eating.

"Yeah, I should be heading out soon," I said, "I'll brush my teeth when I finish breakfast and then I'll be going."

As I was brushing my teeth, I heard a knock on the front door. I assumed it was Harry. My mother then opened the front door and let Harry in.

"Wow," Harry exclaimed in surprise, "Something smells really good in here, Mrs. Marino."

"Oh, well, they're my famous egg omelets," my mother responded, "Next time I make an egg omelet, if you come over a little earlier, you can have some with us."

"Well, thanks, Mrs. Marino," Harry said, "This morning, I just had a bowl of oatmeal with not a lot of flavor, I must say. Oh, and some orange juice with it, that was all."

I had finished brushing my teeth by then, and I headed down to the kitchen where Harry was. We left with our bikes after we both said goodbye to my mom.

***

As we approached the school with our bikes, we noticed Rocco Lombardi talking with Charles Harrison, a friend of mine. Strange how Rocco of all people was talking to Charles.

"Hey, what do you think's going on there, Brian?" Harry asked.

"Well, it can't be good," I said.

As we pedaled past them, Harry and I noticed Charles walking away.

"Hey, kid, where you going?" Rocco said condescendingly.

"Far away from you," Charles responded as he walked away.

"I'll catch up with you later," Rocco said in an angered voice as he began to walk away. We continued pedaling our bikes until we reached the school.

***

As we approached our lockers, across the hall was Jane Reed, with all the boys hanging around her, naturally. I guess she's starting off young with the guys. Nevertheless, we continued walking over to our lockers.

I felt a bit strange asking Harry where my locker was, and Harry looked bewildered when I asked him, too.

"What, you forgot where your locker was?" Harry questioned me.

I could understand why, though. It feels pretty strange when you ask someone that kind of a question.

"Well, Harry," I concluded, "I'm gonna have to head over to the office, 'cause apparently I don't remember my combination either."

"Yeah, I always knew you were crazy anyway," Harry jokingly waved me off as he closed his locker and started walking to homeroom.

After I had received my combination and locker number, as I was heading toward my first class, I walked past George Davis, and his breath smelled a bit like cigarette smoke. As I arrived at my first class, I had to hand the teacher a pass for being late, so he could excuse my absence. After he took the pass, I looked around to see which seat was available, being I didn't know where my seat was. There were two empty seats. Of course, I chose the wrong one of the two, and that's when Mr. Laurier corrected me.

"Hey, Brian," Mr. Laurier said, "Why are you in the wrong seat?"

Of course, many students turned around and stared at me, only adding to the humiliating moment.

"Oh, sorry, Mr. Laurier," I nervously began, "I was thinking of my other class."

"Well, you'd better start thinking," Mr. Laurier said, raising his eyebrow at me, "'cause today's test day."

Oh dear, that helps a lot. I'm not even sure what this whole test is about, but I guess I'll wing it.

"But last week we had a review on this test, so I'm hoping everybody does well," Mr. Laurier said.

Well, it's a shame I wasn't there for the review. I used to be a straight-A student when it came to history, but after this test, I don't think so.

CHAPTER 15

The Faceoff

"Why don't you mind your own business..."

The bell rang, and class was over. "Oh, um, one more thing," Mr. Laurier said to us as we began to leave for our next class, "Make sure to put your tests on my desk as you're leaving. Tomorrow, we'll be starting with the assassination of Archduke Franz Ferdinand, and how that propelled us into World War I."

"Well, I'll see you at lunch," Harry said to me as we walked out. Harry had Mrs. Sullivan for English, and I had Mrs. Handwerger for

English.

"Alright, I'll see you then," I said as we parted ways for our next class.

As I approached my locker, my eyes wandered about the crowded hallway, eventually noticing Charles Harrison walking, with Rocco Lombardi creeping alongside him.

As I looked through the crowd, I couldn't see Charles anymore; my eyes continued to wander about in confusion for a couple more seconds before I recognized Rocco running away.

As Rocco ran past me, I began to approach closer with suspicion. I then noticed Charles lying up against his locker, his books sprawled about the floor.

I proceeded to approach Charles, and helped him up. I gathered his books and handed them to him.

"Is everything alright," I inquired, "What happened?"

"Well, I tripped," Charles said quietly.

"Are you sure it wasn't Rocco who tripped you?" I asked, "I saw him running away."

Charles went silent, pausing for a few seconds before he responded.

"Yeah, well, he tripped me," Charles replied sadly.

"How long has he been bothering you?" I asked.

"Well, since the beginning of this year," Charles said, "It seems to be getting worse."

"Well, I'll walk you to class," I said, "I just have to stop at my locker first."

"Thanks, Brian," Charles said, his voice now sounding more optimistic.

We then both walked together towards my locker, and I gathered the books I needed for my next class, which was English.

After I gathered my books and closed my locker, Charles and I both walked off to our next class, since we both had Mrs. Handwerger for English.

"You know, I'm thinking about getting involved in the school election," Charles said as we walked to class.

"Well, you got my vote," I said.

"Yeah, I'm thinking of taking on the job of...maybe an advisor or Secretary," Charles responded, "Well, I might not be the right person for it, anyway."

"But if you have a dream, you should pursue it," I helpfully suggested.

We then walked off to our next class of the day.

***

We then had Science after English. I came to find out that Jane Reed was sitting at the desk right next to me, me of all people. She would always drop her pencil and expect me to pick it up. There was a point, of course, when I got tired of doing this, but I followed through with it anyway whenever she dropped her pencil again. I don't know if she sees anything in me, but I'm sure she would go for anybody, knowing her. It's probably more flirting than anything else. It just gets on my nerves a little. Maybe I should drop my pencil and see if she'll pick it up for me. But then again, I don't wanna give her any ideas.

***

At the end of Science, the bell rang for lunch. If I remember right, today is Pizza Day in the cafeteria. If I also remember right, the pizza tastes like cardboard with sauce and cheese on it. The food at my school has a reputation for being that way. Well, as long as it's not moving, I guess I'll eat it.
As I walked toward Harry's table with my cardboard-like pizza, Harry saved me a seat. As I began to eat with Harry, Jane walked by and dropped her fork, probably

purposefully.

"Pick it up, Harry," I quietly whispered to him. Harry picked it up, proceeding to hand it to Jane.

"Why would I eat with that fork now?" Jane questioned Harry, staring at him quizzically, then walking away.

"Hey, Brian, why'd you ask me to pick it up?" Harry asked in a serious tone.

"Because I know she doesn't like you," I responded jokingly.

"You know, you're crazy, Brian," Harry said as he sat back down in his seat, "You're really crazy, you know that?"

"I know it," I responded with a smile streaked across my face.

As we ate lunch, we noticed Rocco Lombardi walking up to Charles Harrison as Charles was eating his lunch. Rocco was saying some unintelligible words to Charles, and Charles looked back up at Rocco, appearing irritated by Rocco's presence.

It seemed as if Rocco was starting to get a little bit heated with Charles, and as the conversation got heated, that was when Rocco flipped Charles' food tray over. The tray fell in Charles' lap, and Charles rose from his seat, now facing Rocco.

They faced each other in a confrontation

that went on for several seconds, before Rocco pushed Charles back down on his seat. That was when I got involved.

I then approached the scene, and walked over to Rocco, tapping him on the shoulder. Rocco turned to me.

"Rocco," I began, "why don't you mind your own business and leave Charles alone?"

"Well, it's not your business, that's for one thing," Rocco responded defiantly.

"Well, in this case, I'm making it my business," I then said.

"Well, in this case, don't make things your business," Rocco responded, still facing me.

"Let me give you a word of advice," I began again, still facing Rocco, "If you mess with Charles, you're messing with me."

"Well, then," Rocco concluded with a cool, reflexive raise of the eyebrow as he clenched his fist, and that was when he swung at me. Thank goodness for jiu-jitsu, I blocked his punch with my arm and, after grappling with him for a couple seconds, pulled off an inside-leg takedown on him, tripping him with my leg, which wrapped around his, causing him to fall to the ground. I then proceeded to quickly mount him, then performing an Ezekiel choke; this left him helplessly incapacitated.

The room fell silent when I took down Rocco, but then some of the room broke into chatter, whispering and murmuring to each other about what was happening.

Before getting off him, I proceeded to inch my face closer to his ear, whispering to him. "Before this gets any more embarrassing for you," I whispered, "I suggest we get up and you apologize to Charles, and then we all shake hands. How about that for a deal?"

"Okay, okay, okay," Rocco responded quickly and hurriedly.

I then freed Rocco from the grip I had on him, and we then both got back up, shaking off the embarrassing scene. Rocco then faced Charles, ready to make his apology.

"Well, I'm sorry, Charles," Rocco responded, now in a quiet, softer voice, "Sorry for all the times I harassed you. Well, you could have my lunch."

Rocco slid over his lunch that was on the table to Charles, and Charles then took it, then looked back up at Rocco.

"Thanks, Rocco," Charles said, sitting back down at his seat.

We all shook hands and the matter was resolved.

***

The last bell of the day had rung.

I was heading towards my locker, when I noticed Rocco standing there by the locker, waiting for me. I wondered whether Rocco had any intentions behind this.

"Thanks, Brian," Rocco began in a quiet, introverted voice, "I guess you put me in my place today."

"Yeah, I didn't mean to embarrass you, Rocco," I earnestly replied, "I was just out to protect Charles, and I didn't like the idea of Charles being bullied, and I know Charles didn't like it either."

"Well, I'm trying to fix things about myself," Rocco acknowledged somberly, "and I guess I'm just taking out some frustrations on Charles. I mean, I know I shouldn't be doing that, but that's the way things have been going lately."

"But tomorrow's another day," I suggested reassuringly, "You should make the best of it."

"I'm sure gonna try, that's for sure," Rocco said.

"Hey, Rocco," I said, "I plan on going bowling this weekend. You wanna join me? Charles will be there."

"I don't have any plans," Rocco said, "and I know their pizza's better than the garbage they serve us here."

"I guess it's a deal," I concluded as we walked off.

CHAPTER 16

The Resolution

"I'm considering being a teacher."

I woke up from a dream I was having, and my mother was calling me.

"Brian! Brian, wake up! We've gotta get ready for tonight!"

Tonight? What's tonight? What's going on tonight? Why was I taking a nap, anyways?

"What's going on tonight, Mom?" I inquired from my bedroom.

"What, you forgot?" my mom answered, "It's New Year's Eve! Uncle Bob, Aunt Martha, and your cousin Angela will be coming over soon."

Huh. It's New Year's Eve. I wonder what year it is.

It was New Year's Eve, and my mother's family was coming over our house for the night.

I'm hoping that my Aunt Martha makes one of her really nice cheesecakes to bring over tonight. My Uncle Bob likes to play Scrabble, so we'll have a fun time playing that tonight. I'm sure my mom will make some really delicious appetizers.

But that was a strange dream I just had during my nap. Very strange dream it was, I tell you.

I dreamt I was at this party; I felt like I knew everyone there, I just don't remember their names. I was standing in front of all these people, and somebody—yes, it was a woman—was getting everyone's attention at the podium. I was close to the podium, where she was speaking, and then I remember her saying something about the floor or the floor being all mine or something along those lines. Then the next minute was when everything went black; I felt myself falling, everything spinning, everything out of control at that moment, and then that was when everything went hazy and foggy and then it all went black.

Then I heard my mom—yes, it was my mother—calling me, calling my name, "Brian", "Brian", and she kept calling me. Then I woke up.

**

"Hey, Brian, come here!"
It was my brother Leonard, calling me from his room.
The doorbell rang.
"Brian, get the door!" my mother called.
"Leonard, you're gonna have to wait. I'm on my way, Mom," I answered as I raced downstairs to open the door.
I then opened the door, and my Uncle Bob, Aunt Martha, and my cousin Angela came in. After they had entered the house, I noticed that Aunt Martha had brought some cheesecake for dessert, and my cousin Angela brought some candy-covered popcorn for a snack.
"How's it going, Brian?" Uncle Bob asked in a deep, low-pitched voice.
"Hi, sweetie," Aunt Martha said as she hugged me.
"Hi, cuz," my cousin Angela said, and we both hugged.

"Well, I'm happy you could all be here tonight," I said to them, "I believe Mom is whipping up a special dinner tonight."

"Well, it smells like my favorite," Uncle Bob responded, "I've been trying to get your Aunt Martha to cook me some of that for years."

"Well, it would never come out the way Linda makes it," Aunt Martha said to Uncle Bob, looking over at him.

"What is this that's so special?" my cousin Angela questioned, appearing puzzled.

"It's my mom's favorite meatloaf," I responded, "It's been in the family for years."

"Hey everyone, the appetizers are ready!" my mother called out from the living room. The appetizers were now out, and my father already had his hand in there.

"Mark, get your hand out of there. We have to say grace first," my mother sternly scolded my father.

"Okay, dear," my father politely acquiesced as he took his hand out of the appetizer dish.

"Leonard, come on down!" my mother called.

Leonard came over to where we were, and greeted everyone. After grace was said, we all enjoyed my mother's delicious appetizers.

***

98

We were all busy catching up on things, since we hadn't seen each other for a couple months. Mom was back in the kitchen, checking on the meatloaf, and we spent some time talking to each other as we sat by the appetizer table and picked from the appetizer dish.

"Leonard, what was it you wanted before?" I asked.

"I need help with the project I'm working on," Leonard answered.

"What project is this?" I inquired.

"Don't you remember, Brian? You're the one who gave me the idea," Leonard questioned me, staring at me with a strange look on his face.

"Oh, okay, refresh my memory," I said.

"It's for my school science project," Leonard began, "I'm building a volcano model—a working volcano."

"Oh, yeah, yeah, baking soda and vinegar," I said, "How about if I help you next year?"

"Next year? I can't wait that long," Leonard responded tempestuously.

"It's not even a day away, Leonard," I helpfully reminded Leonard that it was New Year's Eve.

"Yeah, I guess so," Leonard replied, now in a soft, controlled voice.

***

Dinner was over, and we were now playing Scrabble. It was Uncle Bob's suggestion after dinner that we play Scrabble together as a family, but we all enjoyed the game, so we had no problem with it.

We were in the living room playing when Angela and I started talking to each other while everyone else was taking turns.

"What's your New Year's resolution, Brian?" Angela curiously asked.

"I don't know if I'm gonna be around next year," I nervously said, chuckling in between.

"What do you mean by that?" Angela asked.

"Well, a lot of strange things have been happening lately," I shrugged off the matter, "But let's not talk about me, let's talk about you. What's your New Year's resolution?"

I asked her this knowing full well the answer—I remember Angela would always say that she wanted to be a teacher—but then again, I'll have to see how she responds to my question.

"Next year, I'm going into college," Angela responded, "I'm considering being a teacher."

I remember when she said that on this same day—I believe I responded in the usual way, saying "Wow, that's great". Yes, I remember now—Angela always wanted to be involved with the teaching profession somehow, and she would talk about it whenever she came over our house with Uncle Bob and Aunt Martha. I don't know, I just couldn't see her being a teacher. She would be better as a nurse—I could just see her, working with her patients, talking to her patients, interacting with them well, showing compassion to them. I could just see it in her. If I remember right, I don't think she ever became a teacher. I think she worked in a convenience store—yes, now I remember.

"You know," I began, "I could see you being a nurse. I just think you would make a fantastic nurse; you know, you work well with people, you interact well with others. I could just see you being a nurse."

"I mean, I am good with people," Angela paused for a moment, "I'm also good with children."

"Yeah, but when you're a nurse, you could work with adults and children," I responded.

"I'm gonna give it some thought, Brian,"
Angela said assuredly.
"Okay, Nurse Angela," I said, and we both
laughed about it.

***

The game went on for about twenty
minutes, and we then paused for dessert—
and boy, was that cheesecake amazing. After
dessert, we continued the game, with Uncle
Bob inventively inventing new words every
few minutes. Most of these words we
couldn't find in the dictionary, but he
persistently insisted that they were words,
and that they counted as words. Everyone
just laughed and let him get away with it.
We were now stuck on one particular word
that Uncle Bob invented; this word was quite
a strange and bizarre one at that, but we
managed to get past that word, and, upon
finishing the game, talked and interacted,
and before we knew it, it was 28 minutes to
12:00, and that's when—
"Bring out the candy-covered popcorn!"
It was my cousin Angela who announced
this, and that we would now be watching the
television to wait for the ball drop to happen
at 12:00.

My mother turned on the television for us to watch the ball drop, and my father brought out the party poppers.
Before we knew it, the countdown began.
"10!"
"9!"
"8!"
"7!"
"6!"
"5!"
"4!"
"3!"
"2!"
"1!"

Pop-bang! Pop-bang! Pop-bang! Pop-bang! Pop-bang! Pop-bang! Pop-bang!
As we cheer and shout "Happy New Year!"

CHAPTER 17

The Game Room

"Yeah, she's a floozy."

"Brian, Brian! Wake up!"
I woke up to Rocco and Charles staring at me. I found myself comfortably laying on a couch, not exactly sure of where I was. It looked as if we were at the Apple Grove Community Game Room.

"What did you do, doze off?" Charles asked.

"Oh, I guess I'm tired from New Year's and all," I responded wearily as I sat up, still tired.

"New Year's?" Charles asked, looking at me strangely.

"Yes, New Year's," I protested.

"New Year's was several months ago, Brian," Charles said.

"Oh, yeah, I must've been dreaming," I nervously responded, still somewhat confused.

"Come on, let's have some pizza," Rocco chimed in, "That'll wake you up. Pizza's on Charles."

"What do you mean, pizza's on me?" Charles questioned, turning around to face Rocco.

"Well, you lost the pool game," Rocco said, "But I gotta say, you're a really good pool player. And you would've won if I didn't cheat."

"Yeah, I figured you cheated," Charles raised his voice in indignation.

"Alright, I'll buy the pizza," Rocco resolved the matter, "But you're only getting one slice, okay?"

"Okay, children, let's cut the playing in the sandbox," I remarked to the two of them.

We ordered the pizza and sat in the cafeteria that looked over the game room. As we were seated, having our pizza, Harry Ferguson walked over to our table where we were eating.

"Oh, Harry, you're late," I remarked to him as he approached our table.

"Yeah, late as usual," Charles exclaimed.

"Well, I ain't buying him pizza," Rocco said.

"Yeah, that's alright," Harry concluded, "I'm just here to have fun with you guys. Could I have a seat or am I banished?"

"Come on, have a seat, Harry," I called him over to where I was sitting, being there was an extra chair, "Yeah, we're just messing with you."

We had some conversation with each other as we ate our pizza, Harry grubbing a slice off of me, which I was alright with anyway. We kept on talking for a little bit about how the summertime had been going for us.

As we were talking, we noticed Jane Reed walking by us, heading towards a group of guys, naturally.

"Wait, isn't that Jane Reed?" Harry asked.

"Yeah, she's a floozy," Rocco said, "Always hanging out with the guys. I don't know what she sees in them."

"Well, they see something in her," Harry responded.

"Yeah, I hear she puts out," Charles added.

"I mean, this could all just be talk," I responded, "I know she does like to show off with the guys and all, but that doesn't mean she's a floozy."

"It could mean she's a floozy though,"

Charles said.

"Rocco, where did you hear she's a floozy?" Harry asked.

"Well, I can't quite remember who it was," Rocco paused, "But word gets around."

"Ah, let's move on and talk about something else," I concluded, "That's enough about Jane."

We continued talking for several more minutes before we decided to leave the cafeteria for the game room.

***

Clash! Clash!
As the pool balls went bouncing around.

"You're mighty good with that stick there, Charles," Harry chimed in as Charles walked around the pool table.

"I learned everything from my dad," Charles responded as he prepared his next shot.

"Looks like he may clean the slate," I added to their conversation.

"Yeah, that's why you gotta cheat when you play with this pool shark," Rocco added.

Roy then walked past us and we noticed him heading towards the pinball machine, all by himself.

"Hey," I whispered to the others, "why don't we ask Roy to come and join us?"

"Roy?" Rocco looked at me with bewilderment, "Roy's a loner, so he doesn't wanna hang around with anybody. Only a few friends, maybe, but that's it."

"Well, maybe nobody asked," I responded.

"Well, it's getting late," Harry informed us, "I think we should be heading out now."

"What's the matter," Charles questioned Harry, "Is it past your bedtime?"

"I don't wanna be late for dinner, that's all," Harry said, "My mom's making my favorite meatloaf."

"Yeah, I guess we should get going soon," Rocco said, "being that Charles looks like he's gonna clean the slate off anyway."

"Almost done," Charles added, "Eighth ball in the corner pocket."

He made the last shot and we all decided to leave then. As we all began to head out, I noticed Roy, still at the pinball machine, with no one there but himself.

As we left, we noticed Jane, getting into the car with one of the guys she was talking to. As we walked past the car, we rolled our eyes inconspicuously.

"See, I told you she was a floozy," Rocco whispered to us as we walked off.

"Maybe he's just taking her home," I said to Rocco.

It was then that everyone looked at me as if I was crazy.

"Okay, I know you all think I'm crazy," I said, "But, hey, you never know."

We then proceeded to walk home. I wondered what to expect once I returned home, but I hoped life wasn't any different than it had been yesterday. At least I think it was yesterday. It was probably many months ago, as Charles said.

CHAPTER 18

The Park

"Hello, Brian."

As we were walking home from the game room, we passed Hunter's Park, where a concert was taking place.

During the summertime, every Friday night, Apple Grove holds a concert at Hunter's Park. I decided to attend the concert for the night, since I figured I had nothing else to do.

I wonder if my mother and father are expecting me for dinner, though. Maybe I ought to go home now.

"Hey, Harry," I asked, "Are you staying?"

"Heck, no," Harry said, "I'm not gonna miss out on my mom's meatloaf."

"Well, how about you swing by my mom's house on your way home," I asked, "and tell her that I'll be at the concert having a hot dog."

"Okay, I'll let her know," Harry responded as he started to walk off, then saying goodbye to all of us.

Rocco and Charles decided to stay for the concert, but I think they really wanted to stay for the hot dogs. They were mighty good hot dogs, that's for sure. The hot dog vendor was really nice, too; just a nice, friendly person to talk to. He was known for having the best hot dogs in the county.

He called his business "Buddy's Hot Dogs". Everybody called him "Buddy", but I believe his name was Tom. He also had chili that would burn a hole in concrete. I could imagine what it would do to your stomach. I never tried it though. I'm more of a sauerkraut and mustard kind of person.

As the band was playing, Officer Troy was making his rounds, making sure everyone kept in line. Although Officer Troy was a good guy and all, when it came to following the rules and obeying the law, he'd always make sure everyone kept in line. I wonder what's going on between him and Derek Whitman over there. I hope Derek isn't up to any trouble, or maybe Officer Troy is just reminding Derek to stay out of trouble. After all, Derek sometimes had his run-ins with Officer Troy, whenever it came to issues of discipline or following the rules.

I was finishing my second hot dog, and thinking about going back for another. These hot dogs could be pretty addictive. After I finished my second hot dog, I headed over to the refreshments to get a cold drink. I washed down the two hot dogs with some cold water, then started to walk back to where I was.

As I was walking past the cotton candy stand, I noticed, out of the corner of my eye, away from the crowd, that Mr. Johnson was sitting with someone—it was a woman—and he was sharing some cotton candy with her. It's a bit strange how Mr. Johnson of all people would be here at the park watching the concert, much less be here with a woman. Hmm. Could be that he took my advice. I just find it to be quite strange, him being here.

I approached the bench where they were sitting, and I was about to say hello to Mr.

Johnson when—

"Hello, Brian," Mr. Johnson said in a surprisingly delighted voice.

"Hey, Mr. Johnson," I said, "Nice to see you again!"

"So nice to see you as well," Mr. Johnson said, "What have you been doing lately?"

"Well, I was playing at the game room this afternoon," I responded, "and just enjoyed some hot dogs at this concert."

"Oh, yeah, Buddy's Hot Dogs," Mr. Johnson said, "They're the best. Well, I'd like for you to meet my fiancée, Mary."

"Oh, hi, Mary," I said to her, and we both shook hands.

"I gotta say," Mr. Johnson began, "if it wasn't for you, Mary and I would've probably never met. I want to personally thank you for inspiring me that day when I really needed help to get me out of that difficult time I was going through."

"Well, thank you, Mr. Johnson," I replied sincerely, "I just knew you needed some help, and I really wanted to give you some advice, that's all."

"Yeah, I can't thank you enough," Mr. Johnson gratefully responded, "Mary and I met at church. She sings in the choir."

"Wow, that's great," I said, pausing for a

moment, "Well, I wish we could talk more, but my friends are probably wondering where I am."

"Well, it's nice to see you, Brian," Mr. Johnson said, "We'll have to catch up again sometime. The next time I walk by your house, I'll stop by."

"Please do, Mr. Johnson," I said, "We'd be happy to see you."

"Have a good night, Brian," Mr. Johnson said warmheartedly.

"Alright, have a good night," I said as I walked off, waving goodbye to the two of them.

I joined my friends on the grass, where we sat down and watched the rest of the concert.

CHAPTER 19

The Test

"You gotta be kidding me."

"What happened to him?"
"Is he alright?"
"What happened?"
"Wake up, Brian! Wake up!"
"Must've fainted. I hope it isn't anything serious."
"Mom, what happened to Dad?"
"Go get Angela, alright?"
"Angela, come here!"
"Angela!"
"Well, he's breathing."
"Yes, I see him breathing!"

"I believe he'll be okay."

"He should be alright."

"Yeah, he'll be okay."

"Brian! Brian, wake up!"

It was my father calling me.

"We're almost there for your driver's test, Brian! You're sleeping in the car again? You shouldn't have stayed up that late last night!"

As my father called me, I opened my eyes, waking up from the strange dream I had. I was hearing all these voices—yes, they were voices I knew, voices I recognized, and they were talking about me—and they were talking about something that happened to me, that I fainted or something. I don't remember it all, but it was just strange. And what's this about a driver's test that my father's telling me about? I've been driving for over 30 years, so I wouldn't need any driving test. Well, I suppose I might as well take the test anyway. I should ace the test.

"Hey, Dad," I asked, "If I pass, what car will I be getting?"

"Well, Brian," my father said, "for now, you're still gonna use your bicycle."

"But then what's the point of getting a driver's license, Dad?" I questioned him.

"I mean, just in case I want you to get me

some snacks while the game is on," my father said.

We continued talking for a little bit before we arrived at the place. I never felt so confident in my whole life, knowing that I already know how to drive. In three days, I should have my license once they mail the letter saying that I passed.

Three days went by.

"You gotta be kidding me," I said to my dad. It was then that I found out that I failed the road test. My dad scheduled another appointment with the DMV, but the way things have been going, I don't know if I'll be around for the test or where I'll be during the time I'm supposed to take another road test.

CHAPTER 20

The Intervention

"Is it alright if I call you tonight at 8:00…"

His favorite actors, one of his favorite movies, and he's sleeping in the theater. I wonder how much he missed of the movie.

"Brian, get up," I said to him. He started to awake, slowly sitting back up, looking as if he were confused and unsure of where he was.

"Brian, are you alright?" I asked.

"Oh, gee," Brian responded in a low-pitched, weary voice, "Where am I?"

"At the movie theater," I responded.

"What movie are we watching?" Brian asked, still confused.

"The movie you wanted to see all month," I told him in disbelief.

"Harry, is that you?" Brian looked at me in puzzlement.

"Yes, of course, it's me," I raised my voice, agitated yet simultaneously concerned, "Brian, do you even know what day it is and why we're here?"

"Uh, well," Brian paused.

"It's to celebrate my birthday," I said, "How much of the movie have you missed?"

"Yeah, I don't remember any of it," Brian said, still appearing a little confused but now seeming to regain his consciousness.

"You slept through half of the movie?" I questioned Brian.

"Did we have cake yet?" Brian asked.

"No, of course we didn't," I said, "We didn't go over my house yet. We're still watching the movie, or at least, I'm watching the movie."

"Oh, well, I'm sorry," Brian apologetically responded, "I'll be alright now."

"I hope so," I said, "because the best part's coming soon."

We watched the rest of the movie and left

the theater after that. We went over my house to have some pizza for dinner and birthday cake for dessert.

A bit strange, how Brian was acting today. I wonder what got into him. He usually doesn't act like this. He needs cake, that'll straighten him out.

***

I was stuck here since Saturday night, when Harry woke me up at the movie theater. Harry must have thought I was crazy that day by the way I was acting when I woke up. It was a Monday morning, and my dad was about to hand me the keys so that I could drive myself to school. He decided that since it was a nice day, I should probably take my bicycle. Every chance he had he would prevent me from driving the car. In order for me to drive a car I'll probably have to buy my own. In order to do that though, I'm gonna need a better job that pays more.

I rode to school on my bicycle, and as the school day passed by, it was time for lunch. I decided to walk around the school grounds during lunch, and it made for a pretty calm walk, considering the fact that school today was a bit hectic and I needed a break after it all.

***

I just can't take it anymore. Does anyone care? I wish they did. I wish people did care about me more than they do. Well, after all, I do have some friends; at least I have some people to talk to. But if only those friends weren't so out-of-reach, being I don't have classes with them. I mean I guess I get to talk to them sometimes at lunch, but that's about all. Other than that, they're pretty hard to reach, and other than those friends, I don't have much to look forward to, if anything. Me. Roy. Just a loner. Just a dwindling lonely person out of touch with the world. I suppose that's what I've always been. Sometimes you can't help being assigned a role in life. I guess that was the case with me. But I guess in this case, I don't like the role, and I don't like the cards I've been dealt in life. And I wish I could stop pretending that I like these cards that I've been dealt, and that I like my role, because I know deep down that I don't. I know that I don't. Can't it be changed? Maybe it could, but I don't see how.

It's just been a bit rough lately, with all that's been going on, and what makes it worse is the fact that lately I haven't been seeing any light at the end of the tunnel, being that my family doesn't really pay much attention to me, and it's hard to reach out to them being they're so busy with other things sometimes, and it seems like they don't have any time for me; well, I mean sometimes they do, but not when I need it the most. I mean, why live on? What's the point? I see no purpose in living.

**

"Hey, Roy," I came up to him.
"Hi, Brian," Roy responded to me in a soft, downcast voice.
Oh dear. Isn't this the day Roy killed himself? I remember that day. I remember being here too, walking by him, not saying anything to him as I walked by him. Yes, this is the day Roy killed himself.
"So Roy," I began, "How's things going?"
"Why do you ask?" Roy looked up at me, "Does anybody really care how I'm doing?"
"Roy," I responded, "I care. I really want to know how you're doing."

"Let's just say, I feel like I don't belong here," Roy said in a disheartened voice.

"Well, Roy," I began, "I need your help. I really need you to help me."

"Well, what is it?" Roy asked quietly.

"I'm working on a project for the school paper," I said, "I'll be taking some photographs of some upcoming events at the school, you know, special events and all. I'll also be interviewing some teachers and students. I have some equipment that I would need help with.

"I was wondering if you wanted to help out with that," I continued, "and there might also be an opportunity for you to help out with some of the photographs and interviews. It could be a good opportunity for you to get to know more people and see what's going on around the school."

"But why me?" Roy asked, appearing confused.

"'Cause I need somebody that I can trust to be there, and I need someone who I know will work right alongside me," I answered, "and you're that person."

"Well, I really appreciate it," Roy said in a now optimistic voice.

"Is it alright if I call you tonight at 8:00," I asked him, "and we could go over everything?"

"Yeah, that's alright with me," Roy responded in a quiet, reserved voice.

"Yeah, we could talk about it more tonight," I replied, "and I'm glad you're coming aboard. It's really gonna be a help to me, and believe me, you're gonna get something out of this as well."

I paused for a moment as we continued walking around the school. Lunch would be over in ten minutes or so, so I figured we would be heading over to our respective classes soon.

Yeah, I remember Roy. He was a pretty quiet guy, and didn't have that many friends. He always kept to himself, well, maybe not always, but most of the time. I'm hoping that this can help him get through some of the things he's been struggling through.

As we walked along the premises of the school, I was thinking that I should probably ask Roy something else, besides helping out with the photographs and interviews that I was assigned to do for the school paper.

"Hey, Roy," I asked, "This Saturday, I have to shoot some photographs of the outside premises of the school. But I was thinking of stopping at the Stop-n-Go for breakfast. I was wondering if you wanted to come with me for breakfast. My treat."

"Yeah, sure, I'd like to join you," Roy responded in a surprisingly upbeat tone. We walked on and talked a little longer before we decided to walk back into the school building and head toward our classes.

CHAPTER 21

The Discussion

"I guess a hand-me-down is better than nothing."

I woke up on the living room couch, once again, not knowing what day it was. It seems like my dad and I are watching the news, since I believe dinner is over by now.

As we were sitting there, talking about the news, I noticed something show up on the news that I remembered. They were talking about the fire that happened down on Main Street. Took out four or five buildings, from what I recall. If I remember right, they replaced them with a new police station.

A pretty bad fire that was.

Meanwhile, my dad and I were talking for some time about other things besides the news.

"Why is it that we never had a dog?" I asked my father.

"Well, your mom and I were always working on things," my father replied, "and you were at school, so we wouldn't have enough time for the dog."

"Oh, I understand now," I said, "Also, why haven't you decided on having another child other than my brother and I?"

"We had trouble having your brother," he said, "and we were very thankful when we did have you and him as our children, but after your brother was born, your mother was unable to have any more children."

"Oh, I see," I said, "But I have another question. I'd like to have my own car."

"So, how do you plan on getting it?" my father asked with a smirk on his face.

"Well, that's why I'm asking you," I said.

"But money doesn't grow on trees," my father reminded me, "And if it did, I'd have a lot of trees in the backyard and the front yard. However, Mom and I are planning on replacing our car. It's a pretty good-working car, and with some extra work, it could be yours."

"Well, I guess a hand-me-down is better than nothing," I replied, and we both continued to watch the news for a little while before we went upstairs to join my mother and brother, who were already getting ready for bed. I cleaned myself up and got ready for bed.

As I lay down in bed, I thought about all that was going on with me. Will I wake up tomorrow, next week, next month, or next year? Who knows anymore? I'm not even sure of it myself.

CHAPTER 22

The Council

"Maybe that's what he needs."

**STUDENT COUNCIL MEETING – 2:45PM IN
LIBRARY**

I spotted the poster in the hallway of the
school about the upcoming Student
Council meeting that would be
happening today. If I remember right,
Charles Harrison was always interested in
politics, being he would talk about it quite a
bit whenever we talked to each other.
Sometimes he would mention the upcoming
town elections and share his opinions on
political matters. The Student Council could

be a way for Charles to get involved with sharing his thoughts and listening to other people's thoughts. If I could recall, I don't remember Charles amounting to anything in the political world. Maybe I ought to ask him if he'd like to be involved with the Student Council.

INTERESTED IN JOINING THE STUDENT COUNCIL?

TODAY'S THE DAY

2:45PM – LIBRARY

I saw it again. Another sign. Except this one asked if anyone was willing to join the Student Council. Couldn't be a better time than now for Charles to get involved with the Student Council. Maybe I should invite Charles to the meeting. I probably should ask him now. When I see Charles in the lunch room today I'll ask him; I just can't ask him now, being I have an errand to run for my teacher, Mrs. Santiago.
As I walked by the lockers, I headed over to the main office to drop something off for Mrs. Santiago.

STUDENT COUNCIL FUNDRAISER – THIS SATURDAY AT THE STOP-N-GO

DONATIONS WILL GO TOWARD REPAIRING THE SCHOOL CLOCK TOWER

I saw another sign.

Oh, there's Charles. What's he doing out here? Class isn't over yet.

I walked over to Charles as he was walking over to the office.

"Charles, what's going on?" I asked.

"I'm heading towards the restroom now," he responded.

"Well, I need to talk to you during lunch," I told him as we walked along.

"Okay, I'll sit with you," Charles said as he walked over to the bathroom.

WANT TO JOIN A STUDENT LEADERSHIP PROGRAM?

JOIN THE STUDENT COUNCIL LEADERSHIP PROGRAM!

I saw another sign as I continued walking toward the main office.

***

It was lunchtime now, and I was walking to find a table, my lunch tray in my hand, when I noticed Charles Harrison walking behind me. We both walked over to an empty table and sat across from each other. "So Charles," I asked, "you like the pasta here?"

"It's not like Mom's," Charles responded, "but it's not bad either."

"Yeah, I guess it's not that bad," I replied, "but I'm not too keen on it, and I prefer the sausage calzones they make."

We both talked for a little while until Charles asked me what I wanted to talk to him about.

"Charles," I began, "I know you're pretty up on politics and everything. Did you ever think of joining the Student Council? That could be a way to get your name out there. I know it isn't big-time politics, but it could be a launching pad onto something bigger.

"I know you have a lot of knowledge about politics," I continued, "and I know you probably have a desire to get involved in that field. Well, the only way to start is sometimes, you gotta start small. Maybe this is a good way to start. 2:45 today, they're having a meeting in the library for newcomers."

"How did you find this out?" Charles questioned me, appearing mystified.

"Why, there's flyers all over the school," I exclaimed wildly and in disbelief.

"I guess I don't pay attention sometimes," Charles shrugged off the matter, "I might be walking with my head down, and I don't notice."

"Well, you better start noticing," I reminded him again, "'cause it's everywhere. It's even in here. Look, right next to the clock!"

INTERESTED IN JOINING THE STUDENT COUNCIL?

TODAY'S THE DAY

2:45PM – LIBRARY

There the sign was, right next to the clock. I was just joking with Charles, however, being that every now and then, we'll joke around with each other.

"Are you joining?" Charles asked.

"Well, I'm already involved in other school events," I said.

"Well, I'll be there," Charles said, "I'm sure it's something I'll enjoy. Thanks for letting me know."

"Yeah, you're welcome, Charles," I said.

We continued talking for a while before lunch was over and we headed over to our classes. Well, thinking about Charles being part of the Student Council, I think that Charles would do really well. After all, maybe that's what he needs.

CHAPTER 23

The Pool Party

"Well, you know I'm President…"

Underwater. Water flooding my mouth. Rocco pulling me up out of the water. An upturned inflatable float. Choking. Still choking on the water, water that went down my throat, even a little into my lungs.

"Brian, are you alright?"

Rocco asked me as I regained my composure.

"Brian, are you alright?"

Rocco asked again.

"You must have fallen off the float!" Rocco said.

"Now wait, wait a second," I began, my mind

beginning to whirl in confusion, "Where am I now? Rocco, where-where am I?"

"We're at Sally's house," Rocco told me, "We're having a pool party."

"Oh, okay," I said as my confusion slowly went away. I stepped out of the pool, and walked off, still somewhat choking.

Oh, I wonder what day it is now. What time, what month? Okay, I'm at Sally's pool party, but I don't even remember any of this in the past. Strange, isn't it, how you can forget things that happened in your childhood. If they even happened, that is. I guess this was a small occurrence that happened in my childhood, so it probably doesn't mean much that I don't remember it.

I then saw Sally come out and announce that the hamburgers and hot dogs were out on the grill.

"I hope everyone's hungry," Sally said before she walked back into the house.

Hmm. Sally must know a lot of people, being she has a lot of people over her house.

I then noticed Charles and George walking up to me. The two said hello to me, and we talked. I asked Charles how the Student Council was going.

"Well, you know I'm President, Brian," Charles informed me, "Didn't you vote for me?"

"Oh, yeah, I remember that," I pretended to recall, even though I was still struggling to process exactly what he said, "So George, what are you up to?"

"Not much lately," George replied as he took a quick drag from his cigarette, "Just hangin' in there, that's all. Living life by the day. How have you been?"

"Other than having a little water in my lungs," I responded, "I'm hopeful that things will get better, despite the fact that I've been feeling a little disoriented lately."

"Yeah, but I could fix that with a cigarette," George said assuredly, "and not a regular cigarette."

"No thanks, I'll take a pass on that," I said, and we continued talking before George and Charles headed over to where the food was. I then looked around for a couple seconds, eventually noticing Jane Reed and some of the guys she was hanging around with. I also noticed Harry Ferguson walking in, late as usual, but he's always on time for the food. As Harry entered the pool area, he noticed me standing near the pool and walked toward me.

"Hi, Brian," Harry said to me, "Where's the food?"

"Is that all you could think about is food?" I asked, "The first thing you should do when you come here is greet people. Say hi to Sally, or Charles."

"Well, I guess I could say hi to Sally on my way toward the food," Harry responded as he began to walk over to where the food was.

"Okay, I'll be there in a few," I said.

I left the pool area, heading towards the food, and bumped into Derek Whitman, who was at the party, surprisingly. Usually I don't see him at these types of events, being he's a drifter and all.

"Hey, Derek," I said, "How's it going?"

"I've been doing pretty good lately," Derek said, "How have you been?"

"I'm good today," I replied, "I just don't know what I'm in for tomorrow."

Derek gave me a strange look after I said this. We then said goodbye to each other as Derek walked away, heading towards the food.

After we were all filled up from dinner, we decided to go to the park, which was down the street from Sally's house, to watch the fireworks go off and celebrate Apple Grove's centennial.

We got in our cars and drove over to the park to watch the fireworks.

CHAPTER 24

The Drive Home

"Is everything alright?"

S izzle. *Another sizzle.*
Crack. Boom!
Crack. Boom!
Sizzle. A couple more sizzles.
Crack. Boom!
Crack. Boom!
Crack. Boom!
As the firework display went on, we looked on at the brilliant, overwhelming sight of the bright, gleaming fireworks. The fireworks continued to glow, emitting a majestic radiance of light, and we looked on for several minutes as the fireworks

continued. Before the fireworks began, the marching band that played presented quite a spectacular display on the field. And as the fireworks went on, the crowd continued to cheer in awe and wonder at the striking sight that beheld them. It was a dark, moonless night, which made it even better. Everywhere you turned, there were people, people from not only Apple Grove, but the surrounding towns. After the grand finale, things began to settle down. I headed over to my car to head home. After I got in the car, I started driving down side roads to avoid some of the traffic, and noticed Jane Reed walking in the dark by herself.

I pulled over and rolled down the window. "Hi, Jane," I said to her, "Is everything alright?"

"Oh, I'm fine," Jane responded dispiritedly, "I'm just having a bad day, and I'm heading home now."

"I figured you're heading home, but you live on the other end of town," I said, "Would you like a ride home?"

"Well, thank you," Jane said as she was about to get in the car, "That would be nice."

"It's not safe to be walking home alone," I told her in a concerned voice.

"To be honest with you," Jane began, "I just

got dumped by David Butler. He spotted Julie Miller and pretty much fixed his eyes on her and just went off, just left me and went off with her."

"Well, sometimes it's best," I helpfully advised, "You're better off not getting involved with someone like that. Hey Jane, have you ever thought of getting to know someone who's a quiet kid, but at least respects you and doesn't care about his ego?"

"Yeah, I guess I've always went for the popular guys," Jane acknowledged, heaving a saddened sigh.

"It doesn't look like it's working for you though," I said, "Maybe it's best to try the unpopular, you know, the quiet guys, and see what happens. I think you'll notice something very different."

"In what way?" Jane looked at me with squinting eyes and lowered eyebrows.

"Well, he'll probably be more interested in your inward person than your outward," I said.

"Yeah, but I just don't know if I could escape from this," Jane replied, "you know, from who I am."

"Well, who are you really?" I questioned her in a serious but nonetheless gentle voice, "I mean, is what you're doing now really you?

There might be something else inside you that is the real you. Maybe you should ask yourself that question tonight."

"You think you're a counselor, Brian?" Jane asked me in a joking tone, "Well, you're doing a good job."

"I'm just very observant, that's all," I said earnestly, "And I know that there's something else in you that's waiting to come out."

We talked for a few more minutes before arriving at Jane's house, where I dropped her off.

"Well, thanks for the ride, Counselor Brian," Jane thanked me appreciatively.

"Yeah, no problem," I replied with a chuckle, "As long as you got home safe."

As I headed home, I thought about Jane and her situation. I think Jane's a good person on the inside. I just think she gets a little too caught up with the guys, since I've usually seen her hang around with them. I think she likes the attention. That's probably what it is.

What a day this has been. It all started when I woke up underwater, and it all felt so strange since then. Wonder what tomorrow will bring, that is, if there is a tomorrow.

CHAPTER 25

The Interruption

"Sorry, gotta go."

O h-oh, *say can you see,*
By the dawn's early light,
What so proudly we hailed,
At the twilight's last gleaming,
Whose broad stripes…
I woke up on the living room couch, awaking
to the sound of the Star-Spangled Banner.
Looks like a baseball game is starting, I
realized as I gradually regained
consciousness.

"So you ready, Brian?" my father asked me as
he entered the living room, "Mom's bringing
in some of the finest snacks she made."

"Yeah, I'm ready," I replied in a weak, tired voice.

"Okay guys," my mother said as she entered the living room, "I made you your favorite snacks—fudge bites and caramel-covered popcorn."

...o'er the land of the free,
and the home of the brave!
As the crowd cheered.

"Oh, thank you dear," my father said to my mother as he proceeded to sit down alongside me.

"Hey, Dad," I asked him, "Is this a new television set?"

"Don't you remember?" my father looked at me, appearing befuddled, "We both went to Tony's Appliances and picked it out!"

"Oh, okay, I remember now," I nodded along with him, still somewhat confused as to what he was saying.

"Yeah, how could you forget, Brian?" my father questioned me, "We just picked it up last week."

"Well, I guess I'm still waking up out of my deep sleep," I responded, looking down in a moment of quiet embarrassment.

"Well, have some fudge, that'll wake you up," my father said, "I think Mom put some espresso in it."

And you know, this year, the home team's really been on a roll, hasn't it? But the visiting team, on the other hand, I think's gonna give 'em a bit of a hard time, don't you think, Peter? Well, you see, Ryan, I think...

"So what do you think, Dad?" I asked, "Do you believe these announcers?"

"Well, I like Peter," my father responded, "Peter's pretty good with his predictions. Ryan, on the other hand, I'm not a big fan of him. He has a little bit of an ego sometimes."

The game went on for five innings, and the score was Visitors: 10, Home team: 4.

"So, what do you think about Peter now?" I asked my father inquisitively.

"Well, I wouldn't underestimate his predictions yet," my father replied.

"Yeah, but the home team isn't doing very well now," I said concernedly, "I suppose they might do better later on in the game. It's just strange how with the players they've got, they haven't been doing very well in this game."

"People have been saying it's the coaches they have that are making them lose," my father responded as we continued to watch the game.

And it's a foul ball. That makes two strikes now.

And...here's the pitch.

It's a...it's a strike for the home team.

A bit strange how the home team hasn't been doing so well lately. You think they would be doing better than they are now, but I suppose Dad might be right about the issue with the coaches. Then again, I wouldn't know how they did in the previous games, since I haven't been getting the chance to see the other games lately—you know, with me not knowing where I'm gonna be the next day.

Nonetheless, the game was becoming a disappointment for the home team. The game went on for another inning, and it turned out that things got a little better for the home team; it was the bottom of the sixth inning, and the score was Visitors: 10, Home team: 7.

We continued to watch the game as it went into the top of the seventh inning.

And it's getting better for them, isn't it, Peter?

Yeah, things have been slowly improving for the home team, so I'm keeping my fingers crossed about what happens next.

Yeah, I'm thinking you might be right when you say that they just might have a chance at

pulling it off for this game, so I think they just might win this one.
I mean, it's possible they...
It was then that I remembered something—a memory it was—yes, it was a memory, a memory I didn't quite remember very well at first, and my mind slowly circled, circled back, circling back to the time when Derek Whitman—yes, it was Derek Whitman—robbed that store on this same day.
Yes. Derek Whitman. That troublemaker kid I always knew. He was a drifter. Yes. He certainly was.

...and he's up at bat now, it's the first pitch...
And as that announcer kept talking, and as that game kept playing, my mind circled back to the time when that troublemaker kid Derek Whitman robbed that liquor store and stole some money from it—yes, I remember it was quite a sum of money he stole—not a lot, but enough to fill his pockets.
And it was then that I realized that while—

...and it's a strike for the visiting team again, their second strike it is now...
—while I sat in that living room, alongside my father, having some fudge bites with him, and while those announcers were talking, deliberating over which team would win, it was then that I realized that it was at

that same time that Derek Whitman was driving over to the liquor store he was going to rob—

…and he's going up at bat now, wonder how he's gonna do this time, being he…
—and the announcers continued to talk and deliberate, when I quickly jumped out of my seat in a moment of surprise and shock, surprise and shock at what would now be happening, what would be happening in a matter of minutes.

I quickly walked out of the living room, approaching the door, when—

"Where are you going, Brian?" my father asked me in confusion.

"Sorry, gotta go," I quickly responded.

"But you're missing the game, Brian," my father questioned me, now incredulous.

"I'm not missing anything," I said as I began to walk out. If I recall, the home team does win this game—

…and it's the second pitch now. Bases loaded.
"You're gonna miss the end, Brian!"

…and he throws the pitch…
I ran over to the coat hanger, looked for my coat—

"You're missing it!"

…and he hits it!
"You're missing it, Brian, do you realize

152

that?"

"Sorry, gotta go."

—and I began to put on my coat and—

...it looks like...it could be out of the park!
—I struggled to get my coat on—

...and he's running...
—still struggling—

...still running...
—struggling to get my coat on—

...passes first base!
"Brian, you're missing it!"

"Wait a sec, I gotta focus here."

...and he's almost at second base now...
—focusing on my coat—

...and he passes second base!
—trying to look at the screen, looking back at my coat—

...and he's approaching third base...
—got my coat on—

...and he passes third base!
—tripping on the rug—

...and he's approaching home plate now!
—regaining my balance, getting back up from the floor—

...and he reaches home plate!
"Brian, you missed it!"

—I quickly opened the door—

"Brian, you missed it, do you realize that?"

...and it's a grand slam for the home team!

—I closed the door—
"Brian, get back here!"
—and took off, realizing I had missed it.

CHAPTER 26

The Prevention

"Why should ya care?"

Should I do the hair salon, or the liquor store? I guess I'll do the liquor store. It's quieter in there.
I'll wait for everyone to leave. Looks like there's a couple customers in there now. So once they get out of there is when I could go in. Should probably wait in the car a little longer.
There goes one of the customers now, getting in his car. Just wondering when the other one's gonna get out. Hopefully no more customers pull into this lot.

There's the other one. He's leaving. Now I could move in.

***

There's Derek's car. I see him in it. I'll park on the other side. Better make sure to encounter him at the door. I'm sure he's not gonna see me pulling in.

***

Well, I suppose I should be getting on with this. I may as well do this now, being I don't see any customers in there.

***

I wonder whose car that is. It's been parked out there for quite some time. Looking out the window now. Haven't seen anybody get out yet. But I see someone in there. They still haven't gotten out. Well, I ought to keep stacking these liquor bottles now, and see if he's still there in a few minutes. If so, I'll probably have to call the police, but I ought to wait now.

***

He's getting out. Derek's getting out of the car now. Should probably encounter him now.

***

Walking, walking up to the door, approaching it, still approaching, ready to open it, somebody stops me, is that Brian, yes, it's Brian.

"Hey, Derek," Brian said, "I know what you're trying to do here. It's not right. You shouldn't be doing this."

"Would you step away?" I asked, irritated.

"No, I'm not moving, Derek," Brian continued to face me, "If it's money you need, I got $35. You could take it if you want to, but just don't go in there and rob the store."

"This matter don't concern you, okay," I answered, "Why should ya care?"

"Because I know what you're doing, Derek," Brian confronted me as he prevented me from entering, "Robbing people's homes, and now you're gonna do stores. This could only get worse, Derek. How long you think you're gonna get away with this? This could only lead to jail time. Please, promise me you're not gonna do anything like this."

"But I still don't understand, Brian," I said, "Why should ya care?"

"Because I'd hate to read the newspaper and see your name on a police report," Brian responded in a serious tone.

"All right," I gave in, "I'll lay off on this for the time being, but you better have something good to say now."

Brian offered me to have dinner with him so that we could talk.

CHAPTER 27

The Meeting

"A minimum-wage job?"

Derek and I went over to Triple Ps, Patsy's Pizza & Pasta. Derek got himself a chicken parmesan dish, and I got the spaghetti Bolognese. We also had some garlic bread; it's known to be the best garlic bread in the city of Apple Grove, and of course, it was really good.

As we were talking for a while, I started to encourage Derek to work on getting his act together and cleaning himself up once and for all, in terms of some of the criminal activity he's gotten himself caught up in lately.

"What, do you want me to get a job?" Derek questioned me, "A minimum-wage job?"

"No, not a minimum-wage job," I responded, "A decent-paying job."

"How do you expect me to get a decent-paying job?" Derek asked, "I don't have much experience in anything."

"Well, I've seen you work on cars before, Derek," I said, "and you seem to be pretty good at it. You could always be a mechanic."

"Yeah, but I don't think people are gonna want to hire me," Derek replied disconsolately, "you know, with them knowing my background."

"You could always join the military," I attempted to encourage him again, "You know, you can get an education in the military, and you can get paid while you're doing it. Free healthcare's another benefit, and you also get free food and board. It's not a bad job, either. You're serving your country."

"Then, why don't you join the military?" Derek said.

"Well, I'm planning on going to school for finance," I replied, "I just always thought finance was a more interesting career for me, something that would work well for me."

"I see what you mean," Derek acknowledged, "But I just can't see myself making a career out of the military."

"You don't have to make a career out of it," I said, "Just learn, get the training, do your time, and then once you're out, you'll be able to get a better job. Maybe you could even be a police officer."

"Oh, yeah," Derek replied dismissively, "I don't think Apple Grove would hire me. I'd have to leave here, go somewhere else where people don't know me."

"You know, cops make pretty good money," I said, "They do have good health benefits, and I believe they have a pension when they retire. Promise me that tomorrow, you'll go to the army recruiting center and just listen to what they have to say. I think it will be good for you and your future, because there's no future in what you're doing now. The only future you'll have in crime is in a jail cell."

"Okay, Brian," Derek thanked me, promising that he would stop by the army recruiting center and see what they had to say.

"Alright, Derek," I replied, "I hope you keep your word. Call me tomorrow and let me know how everything worked out."

We continued to talk for a little while before we left Triple P's and parted ways.

CHAPTER 28

The Plans

"Believe me on this one…"

"**B**rian, you're going off the road!" I woke up to the voice of my brother Leonard, finding myself behind the wheel of a car. I quickly regained control of the wheel, managing to steer the car back onto the road after a brief moment of shock at what was happening.

Leonard was looking at me with a disconcerted look on his face, and I noticed this when I looked at him, before turning my eyes to the road again.

"Brian," Leonard began, "You're sleeping behind the wheel? Are you gonna sleep in the movies as well?"

"Oh, I'm sorry, Leonard," I apologized nervously, "I'll be up for the movie. What is it we're going to see?"

"The movie we've been talking about all week," Leonard informed me, sounding confused as to why I was asking.

"Alright, whatever," I replied.

We continued to talk for a little while as we drove to the movie theater, and it was then that Leonard and I began to talk about Leonard's future career in stunt work.

"You know, Brian," Leonard said, "I think I've abandoned the whole stunt work thing. I'm finished with it. I think it's too risky for me. I just don't think it would work for me. I need a profession that's much easier, and much safer at that."

"Hey Leonard," I began, "I have a premonition."

"Oh yeah, you and your premonition," Leonard responded in a joking way, "I still remember the day Dad was driving us to that gas station, and you convinced Dad with your premonition to go to the other gas station 'cause you said it was cheaper, and you were wrong on that."

"Oh, please, forget about that premonition," I brushed it off, "Just believe me on this one, okay? I honestly think you would be really good as a lawyer. Couldn't really see you being a stuntman anyway. I mean, especially when you struggled with riding your bike."

"But isn't it hard to be a lawyer?" Leonard asked.

"Well, think of it like this," I began, "It may be hard at first with the schooling, but being your grades are so good, I don't see it being a problem for you to become a lawyer. The pay's not bad either."

"I guess I could look into it Brian," Leonard replied in a slightly unsure voice, "I probably should try to look into it."

After a few more minutes of talking, we arrived at the movie theater.

As I was paying for the tickets, I noticed Leonard looking somewhat uncomfortable as he looked over at the girl who worked at the concession stand. I picked up some popcorn at the concession stand, and Leonard went to pick out some good seats in the theater.

I noticed Leonard sitting in the middle row when I entered the theater. I went over to sit with him, and rested the bag of popcorn between us. The commercials were beginning, so it would be another ten or fifteen minutes before the movie began.

"Hey Leonard," I began, "You seemed uncomfortable as you looked over at that girl at the concession stand."

"Yeah, she goes to my school," Leonard replied, "I kinda like her. I always thought she was a nice girl to talk to."

"But do you talk to her?" I asked.

"Well, sometimes I get a little nervous and shy," Leonard responded, his posture slouched and his expression downcast.

"Does she ever say hi to you?" I asked.

"Sometimes she does," Leonard said, "I guess my response is a little too quiet, and she's probably over there thinking I'm a dud after hearing my pathetic response."

"You know what I'd do if I were you, Leonard?" I then posed to him, "I would think about what I'm going to say. Then, I would approach her and ask her how she's doing and be prepared to talk with her. The whole key is you need to be bold. And sometimes all you need to do is listen.

"Why don't you go to the concession stand now," I continued, "and get some snacks? And while you're up there, ask her how she's doing, being the commercials are gonna go for a while."

"I don't know about this, Brian," Leonard sighed discontentedly, "I'll probably wind up making a fool of myself."

"Well, if you don't say anything now," I reminded him, "you probably won't ever say anything."

"Okay, I'll do it," Leonard reluctantly answered, beginning to get up out of his seat, "But I'll probably look like a fool anyway, Brian."

Brian was always like this. Always the encouraging type. Now it's time for me to put on the clown show I usually put on, and likely make a fool out of myself in the process. I just always found it difficult when it came to talking to girls; it's like I'm more comfortable talking to the friends I've been with for a while now, you know, friends like Murphy, Andrew, Thomas; I've known them for years. I guess I've just found it hard to connect with a girl, and I usually only say a few words to some of the girls I see at my school. Well, I usually narrow the words down to "hi", whenever the girl says "hi" to me. It's usually a quick "hi" in a low tone. They probably think of me as a dud because of that. I'll have to try to fix things this time, that is, if I can fix things. I've been trying to fix things for a while now, but this time, I'll try to at least say "how are you doing" rather than just "hi".

As I was approaching the concession stand, I noticed that, surprisingly, there weren't a lot of people there. Only a few kids were there, and I just had to wait until they were finished ordering their snacks. It's bad enough that I have anxiety, and it doesn't help that waiting only adds to the anxiety. As I approached the counter, the manager called Susan over to add more butter to the popcorn machine. The manager then walked over to where I was standing, now that the kids had walked off with their concessions. Boy, what are the odds of this happening? I'd better come up with a quick excuse to delay this.

"What would you like?" the manager asked me.

"Well, I'm still not sure yet," I replied, somewhat stressed, "I'm gonna need more time."

As I delayed as long as I could, searching about the concession stand, appearing as if I were uncertain of what I wanted, Susan arrived back at the counter, and I looked back up to find her standing there.

"Oh, hi, Susan," I said, "How are you?"

"Oh, I'm doing really good," Susan's face started to light up as she said this, "How are you, Leonard, and what could I do to help you?"

"Well, I'm here with my brother," I responded, "and I was wondering what you would recommend for a snack, being I've been trying to figure out what I could get for the both of us."

"Well, I just added some fresh butter to the popcorn," Susan replied, "And the popcorn is great. Plus, it's better for you than the candies we have."

"Alright, I'll take a large popcorn," I decided, and she then began to prepare the popcorn box for me.

"Well, you made a good choice," Susan said as she was almost finished preparing the box of popcorn.

I then paid her for the popcorn.

"I hope you enjoy the popcorn and have a great day," Susan said.

"Thank you, Susan," I replied, "I'll see you in school."

"Yeah, I'm looking forward to seeing you in school," Susan said, and I then walked off in disbelief as to what was happening before me. Now I'll be a wreck all weekend, wondering what I'm gonna say to her when I see her in school. Well, I guess my brother was right on this—it's just other things that he gets wrong, like his premonitions.

I walked back into the theater to sit with my brother, now curious as to whether this was a premonition of his or not.

"Was this a premonition of yours, Brian?" I questioned him, still in disbelief.

"What do you mean? What premonition?" Brian asked, appearing confused by what I said, "So what happened at the concession stand?"

"Well, let's just say," I replied in uncertainty, "she seemed like she was happy to see me, and she was nice enough to suggest the popcorn that she just freshly buttered."

"You got a large popcorn?" Brian questioned.

"I didn't know what to say, Brian," I replied sincerely.

"How much change do I get back?" Brian asked.

"Well, I had to get a few dollars out of my pocket as well," I answered, "But she did say that she's looking forward to seeing me at school."

"Well, next time you go to the movies," Brian said, "maybe you'll be going with her."

"Is this one of your premonitions?" I asked.

"I guess we'll find out," Brian shrugged, "Now eat your popcorn. The movie's starting."

CHAPTER 29

The College

"Who knows if I'll ever get back?"

An elevator door opened, and I entered the hallway.

To my recollection, this is the floor that my dorm room is on. I guess I'm in college now. Might as well face the music. See what adventures I'm in for this round. As I walked towards my dorm room, I noticed my roommate, Peter Earnley, coming out of the dorm. He noticed me and we said hi to each other. He said he was stopping at the store to pick up some snacks and asked me if I needed anything. I said no thanks and told him I would just rest for a while.

Peter Earnley. I'd probably starve to death in college if it weren't for him. He was from a very wealthy family, and always brought food into the dorm. If he hadn't done that, I probably would have died in a few weeks. Whenever he ordered food, he'd always order extra for me. The only thing I was able to offer back was to help him with his math. He wasn't great at algebra, and he especially wasn't great at calculus. He was pretty good in geometry, so I'd give him credit for that. He was especially good when it came to subjects like English and History. I would say English was his best, being he could recite any monologue from Shakespeare's *Hamlet*, forward and backward. Particularly Prince Hamlet's "to be or not to be" monologue.

As I rested for a little while in the room, I was still trying to figure out why I was placed here, of all places. I surely don't need to help Peter. He's got everything he needs. It's just that I find it a little strange that I find myself in a college dorm room when I could be anywhere else but here. Then again, who knows?

Who knows if I'll ever get back? Get back

after this situation. And perhaps the many other situations that'll ensue after this one? Maybe I'll get back sometime. I don't know. Sometimes I find myself forgetting where I came from even when I spend time thinking it over. It's like I find myself spinning, spinning and continuing to spin in a circular motion. Perhaps it is my mind spinning. Sometimes it feels that way, that is. My mind spinning, and my mind wandering, pondering whether this is reality. Or perhaps it is all just a fantasy I find myself occupied with. Reality or not, who knows?

Several hours later, I decided to take a walk around the campus, just to get some air, which I found to be refreshing in the midst of the confusing questions I found myself preoccupied with in the dorm room.

As I was halfway through my walk, I ran into George Davis, who was outside smoking a cigarette, and we both said hi to each other. We then walked together and talked for a little while.

I then remembered. George did go to the same college I went to. I don't think he ever finished college. Probably became occupied with other issues of his own. Couldn't focus on school as a result of that.

CHAPTER 30

The Break

"I think you're going a little too far..."

Several days later, I was on school break, but nonetheless at the college. I was walking from my dorm room to get to the library, which was a building away. When I was outside, as I approached the library building, I noticed George coming out, carrying something in his hand.

***

How could I go on? Life is tough. If it wasn't for these pills I don't know what I would do.

I surely wouldn't be in college if my parents didn't push me to go. And it's not that I don't like my parents or anything. It's not that. I think they have good intentions and everything. It's just that I don't even know what I want to be, what I want to do with myself at this point and it bothers me. It really bothers me. The only thing that keeps me going is these pills. Really. It's the only thing. Oh boy. Here's Brian. I think he noticed me with these pills.

"Hey, George," Brian said as he approached me, "I know you've been smoking lately, but I think you're going a little too far with the pills now."

"Yeah," I replied, "Well, it's the only thing that keeps me on my toes."

"Well," Brian began, "I've been dealing with a lot of things in my life as well, so I could relate to what you're saying. But I don't need that stuff to keep me on my toes."

"So then what do you do?" I asked.

"I do things other than that," Brian said, "like I make sure that I get enough sleep, and I try to stay healthy."

"Yeah, but I mean, come on, Brian," I said, "I'm the one that's got college work that I'm not even used to."

"You think I'm not struggling with things

too?" Brian said, "I'm dealing with a bunch of stuff too. But I'm not turning to pills. Now, if you need any help with college work, we could always study together. You could study with me and I'll help you."

"Yeah, I didn't know you were a calculus expert, Brian," I teased.

"Actually, I do understand calculus quite well," Brian said, "sure, I'm not Einstein, but I have gotten several A's in calculus. Now don't ask me to help you with any art, 'cause I'm a terrible drawer. But just promise me not to take any of those pills anymore. That stuff's not helping you, George. It's really not."

"Alright, Brian," I replied reluctantly, "I mean, it's gonna be hard for me, but I'll give it a try. It'll save me money as well."

"So," Brian said, "do you have any plans tomorrow?"

"No plans at all," I said.

"How about we meet here tomorrow at 10:00," Brian suggested, "spend a few hours, then grab a bite to eat?"

"I suppose we could do that," I said.

"I also have plans on getting a haircut tomorrow," Brian said, "Does it look like I need a haircut?"

"You're asking me, Brian?" I questioned,

"You're asking someone who's got hair past his shoulders?"

"When was the last time you got a haircut?" Brian asked.

"I cut my own hair," I said, "I go right across the bottom, and it's done."

"I've known that you've always had long hair, as long as I can remember," Brian said, "But what you need to do is change your hairstyle. Because changing your hairstyle could help you change other things as well, like your addiction to pills."

"I don't believe that," I answered with a dismissive chuckle, "I mean, how is it that me changing my hairstyle is gonna help me stop taking pills, Brian?"

"Well, if you can be bold enough to change your hairstyle," Brian said, "then you can be bold enough to stop taking pills. It's kinda like, if someone wanted to impress another person, they may dress up and present themselves differently to that person."

"Well, let's work on the pills now," I jokingly remarked, "The hair's for another time."

We continued to talk as we walked about the campus.

***

I was thinking of Abigail. As George and I continued to walk around the campus and talk, I couldn't help thinking about tomorrow and getting to meet Abigail at the salon, where she would cut my hair. I pray everything goes right tomorrow. It's just the idea of losing her of all people, that idea which haunts me. But then again, I don't even know where I'll be tomorrow, so that's another thing to worry about. It's like everything seems so unreal. Even this moment. Even the *now*. Even my conversations with people. My conversation with George. Other people I talk to. On top of that, my inner thoughts I find myself experiencing. It all feels so unreal. Perhaps surreal. If anything out of all of this that I am going through can go right, I pray that it goes right with Abigail tomorrow.

CHAPTER 31

The Salon

"I prefer to wait."

A busy afternoon at the Cutting Edge Salon.

Sounds of blow dryers, scissors, and chatter ring through the fragrant, perfumed air. Hairdressers and manicurists work earnestly, while nonetheless demonstrating the skill of communication with their clients. Meanwhile, a woman, DIANE, stands at the front desk, greeting customers, learning of their requests and needs, then directing them to the waiting area, where coffee and cookies are provided.

181

ENTER: BRIAN MARINO. He opens the salon door, approaching the front desk. He is impressively dressed for the occasion, hoping to find ABIGAIL working at her station.

> DIANE
> *(smiling)*
> Welcome to the Cutting Edge. How can we help you?

BRIAN quickly shifts his eyes to the hairdressers' stations. He notices that ABIGAIL is not among the group of hairdressers. He quickly turns his eyes back to DIANE.

> BRIAN
> Do you know if an Abigail Perkins works here?

> DIANE
> Yes, but she took a late lunch and should be back in about ten minutes.

> BRIAN
> *(shrugging)*
> I'll wait for Abigail.

> DIANE
> *(confused)*
> Well, do you know Abigail?

182

BRIAN
I mean, I have heard from people that she is
very good at hairdressing.

DIANE
The thing is, Abigail has two more
appointments, and one's a color. That's gonna
take some time. But if you're looking to get a
haircut, Patricia's available now.

BRIAN
Eh...I prefer to wait.

DIANE
(pointing to the waiting area)
Well, take a seat in our waiting area. There's
coffee and cookies.

BRIAN
Alright, thank you.

BRIAN walks over to the waiting area, finds
himself a seat, and helps himself to a magazine,
along with some cookies to serve as a
comforting accompaniment.

Still pondering his appointment with ABIGAIL,
hoping it is a success, BRIAN, in the middle of
having his first cookie, notices that these

cookies taste very similar, or, if not, exactly like the ones ABIGAIL would bake for him and the children, when they would enjoy movie nights together, or when they would celebrate the holidays together.

BRIAN also remembered that everyone loved the taste of her chocolate chip cookies, or perhaps, not only the taste of those, but the taste of her oatmeal cookies, and it was then that BRIAN found himself coming back to those days, those memories, and he imagined that he was there, in the living room with ABIGAIL and the children, smelling the sweet and hypnotic aroma that emanated from the platter of cookies.

It was then that BRIAN found himself waking out of his nostalgic memory that was triggered by the sight, smell, and taste of the cookies. It felt like hours to BRIAN, but in fact, it was only a matter of minutes before ABIGAIL entered the waiting area, approaching BRIAN.

ABIGAIL
Are you Brian?

BRIAN
Yes, ma'am, I am.

ABIGAIL
(chuckling)
Well, what makes me so special to you?

BRIAN
Well, I heard you were a really good
hairdresser, and I would like to find out for
myself.

ABIGAIL
Yeah, my two appointments canceled, so I could
take you now. But if my two appointments
didn't cancel, then you would still be willing to
wait here all this time, just for me to give you a
haircut?

BRIAN
(jokingly)
Well...I've got a premonition.

ABIGAIL
(curiously)
Oh...a premonition. Okay then. By all means,
have a seat.

ABIGAIL directs BRIAN to his seat, and BRIAN sits down.

ABIGAIL
How would you like your hair cut?

BRIAN
How about if we leave it up to you?

ABIGAIL
Wow! You're trusting that I'm gonna make the right decision on how you would like your hair styled?

BRIAN
I guess I trust you, that's all.

ABIGAIL
(confused)
Why, you don't even know me.

BRIAN
(reflexively)
Well, by the end of this haircut, I'd like to get to know you.

ABIGAIL widens her eyes in a moment of surprise, before turning to her set of tools,

deciding on the kind of haircut she will give
BRIAN.

BRIAN
So, Abigail, how did you learn to cut hair?

ABIGAIL
(beginning to cut BRIAN's hair)
I've been interested since I was eight. I really
started by practicing on my younger sister's
dolls. I would cut their hair sometimes, and
that was just my way of practicing how to cut
people's hair. I figured, if I learned how to cut a
doll's hair, I would be able to cut a real person's
hair and I would be able to do it right.

ABIGAIL
(cont.)
One day, I became really bold, and cut my
sister's hair. My mom got mad at first, but then
when she realized the job came out so good, and
it saved her money on getting haircuts for my
sister, she not only let me continue to cut my
sister's hair. It ended up being I was cutting
everyone's hair. It got to the point when I
started asking for money. I feel bad about that
now, and I think I got a little greedy at that

187

point. As I got older, I went to a nine-month hair salon school program. Now I work here full-time.

And as ABIGAIL and BRIAN continued to talk, BRIAN asking ABIGAIL questions, ABIGAIL asking BRIAN questions, BRIAN realized, at that moment, that everything was going well, everything was going exactly the way he wanted it to go, and he wished, and kept on wishing, that this moment would not end, knowing that he could be anywhere at any moment, not knowing where he could be next.

As the haircut was coming to an end, BRIAN complemented ABIGAIL on the job she did.

ABIGAIL
It's been a pleasure cutting your hair and talking with you.

BRIAN
Well, let's not say "goodbye". Let's just say "see you later".

And as BRIAN said this, he wished, and he hoped, that they would indeed see each other later.

CHAPTER 32

The Dorm Room

"I should've got her number."

Walking back to my dorm, I couldn't stop thinking of Abigail, wondering if I would ever be with her again. I should've got her number. I'm just going through this cycle that doesn't seem to end—it's really starting to get to me now—and it almost feels like I'm phasing in and out of reality. I don't know what reality is anymore.

Was I ever with Abigail? I don't know. Was I ever married to her? I don't know that either. Or was that a dream? Another one of my fantasies I had? Perhaps this is reality.

Perhaps this is the life I'm truly living. But then how would I know that I was married to her?

It just confuses me. This whole dreaded situation. I can't understand some of these things anymore, but maybe I wasn't meant to. Maybe it's the reality I can't understand. Maybe it's the reality I can't accept, the life I'm truly living, a life without Abigail. Or could it be the dream I'm living? Or should I say "nightmare"?

I'm gonna have to get more haircuts, and maybe I'll be bold enough to ask her for her number. Well, wait a minute. I think I may remember the number, if it's the same. But then if I called, she would wonder how I got the number. It wouldn't make sense to call then. I'm just gonna have to get the number, even though I already think I know it.

I'm driving myself crazy over this. It's probably best I just stop thinking about this whole thing.

***

I entered my dorm room to find a note from Peter, my roommate. The note read:

Hi, Brian.
I'm flying out to get together with my parents
for a few days. I filled up the refrigerator with
groceries for you. I left $20 on the counter, just
in case you need some extra cash for gas or
something else. Sorry for the late notice.

Enjoy your break.
Peter

That Peter's something, I'll tell you. I don't
know if I'll ever be able to pay him back.
Well, before I call my parents to see how
they're doing, I'd better make dinner now,
since there's so much in the refrigerator.

***

It's a choice between chicken francese, mac
'n' cheese, meatloaf, eggplant parmesan, or
fettuccini Alfredo. I guess I'll stick with the
eggplant parmesan; that seems like the best
choice to go with.
I remember when my mom made eggplant
parmesan for us, and whatever she did, the
eggplant always came out so tender and
delicious. When we were very young, my
mom would always say that eggplant came
from chickens. I could never understand her

on that one. Could it be because chickens lay eggs? I don't know if I could answer that question. Maybe I don't know a lot about chickens. But yeah. I always remember when we would joke about that at the dinner table. Whenever we talked about it at dinner, I would ask her, "If eggplant came from chickens, then where did eggs come from?" She would answer with: "Well, eggs came from the Easter Bunny." And then I would say, "Are you saying that rabbits lay eggs?" Then, she would respond with, "Oh, just eat your food before I lay an egg."

Well, I'd better try out this eggplant parmesan. See if it matches my mom's.

***

The eggplant parmesan was pretty good. I wouldn't say it was as good as my mom's, but it was pretty good.

I'm sure my mom and dad are finished with dinner. Should probably give them a call now, before I have that apple pie that Peter left me.

***

I made the call to my family. It went really

well. I got talking to them about some things that have been going on lately, in terms of college. After I told them about my experience in college, I started talking to my brother Leonard, and I asked him how he had been doing. He talked a little bit about him starting to get interested in law, after he had read a couple books on it.

I think I'll have a slice of that apple pie Peter left me.

CHAPTER 33

The Gift

"Have you ever had déjà vu?"

Ring-ring! Ring-ring!
Went the telephone.
Ring-ring! Ring-ring!
Awaking out of sleep to the telephone.

Ring-ring!
The sounding of the telephone. Reaching
out. Hitting the alarm clock.

Whack! Whack! Whack! Whack!
Realizing it was the telephone and not the
alarm clock that was ringing.

Ring-ring! Ring-ring!
Reaching to grab the telephone. I answer the
phone in a groggy voice.

"Hellooooooooooooo…"

"Hey, sleepyhead," a girly voice says to me, "Just reminding you about our dinner reservations tonight."

"Wait. Who's this?" I ask.

"WHO'S THIS?! It's ABIGAIL! What, were you expecting another girl to call?"

"Oh, oh, okay, Abigail," I shakily say, "I-I-I-I'm sorry, I was in a deep sleep. I don't even know what day it is."

"What is that college doing to you?" Abigail says, "Don't you know we have our Valentine's dinner tonight?"

"Oh, yeah, I'm sorry, I'm so confused," I calmly collect myself, "What time are the reservations?"

"6:30 tonight," Abigail reminds me.

"Ok, I-I probably could use a little more sleep," I say.

"It's 11:30am," Abigail says, "Do you need to see a doctor? Why are you so tired?"

"I don't know," I weakly reply as I wearily wake out of bed.

"Well," Abigail replies, "I'm expecting you to pick me up at 6:00pm. Now get back to bed, sleepyhead."

I hang up the phone. I wobble out of bed, heading towards the kitchen, deciding on whether I should have breakfast or lunch. I guess I'm 19 years old. Must be my first Valentine with Abigail. I didn't even get her a gift. Or at least flowers. Could've gotten flowers for her. I don't have time to eat. I've gotta go out to get her something.

It's best that I head out to the store now. See what they have for a Valentine's Day gift.

⁎

I check the time.

5:32pm.

I must go out to pick up Abigail now. She's about a 15-minute ride away, so it shouldn't take too long. Glad I was able to get those gifts. It would've been curtains if I hadn't gotten those gifts. I hope I make it to the dinner with Abigail. Wouldn't want to get transported to another time. That's for sure. Must keep one's fingers crossed. From what I remember she ordered the lobster and I ordered the ribeye. And knowing Abigail she'll definitely want to say grace before we eat. So I think it would be a good idea for me to suggest that. It'll give me some brownie points, that's for certain. I remember the last time this dinner happened the baked potatoes were kind of bland. This time I might not order the baked potatoes.

Probably best not to. And the last time this dinner happened was the first time. I just happen to be experiencing this all over again. Can't understand why. Perhaps I'm not meant to understand it.

Perhaps it's best I get going now.

***

"Why is it that I somehow had a premonition that you were gonna order the cheesecake?" I asked Abigail as she was enjoying her dessert.

"Who do you think you are, some kind of a mind-reader?" Abigail quizzically questioned, "And yes, you're right, I do like cheesecake."

We paused in our conversation for a couple seconds, and continued enjoying our dessert, Abigail enjoying her cheesecake, me enjoying my chocolate mousse.

"Have you ever had déjà vu?" I abruptly asked as I took my last spoonful of chocolate mousse.

"Not recently," she replied.

"Well, lately I've been having déjà vu a lot," I began to elaborate, "It feels like this whole day is déjà vu, honestly."

"But it's our first Valentine's Day dinner, Brian," Abigail reminded me.

"Well," I replied, "I pray it ain't our last."

"What do you mean by that?" Abigail asked.

"Well," I paused momentarily, "I hope I can have more Valentine's Day dinners with you."

"Did you know," Abigail began, "that flowers are the way to a woman's heart? So I want to thank you for that beautiful bouquet of flowers you gave me earlier. My mother also appreciated the flowers you gave to her. Are you trying to get to her heart as well?"

"Well, I-I," I paused, attempting to conceal nervous feelings, "well, you see."

I paused again, gathering my thoughts, thinking of a way to change the subject and, upon doing so, noticed the waitress walking by our table.

"Oh, ma'am," I called out to her, and she turned to face me, "May I have the check please?"

"Yeah, sure," the waitress answered as she began to walk off.

"Boy, that ribeye was good," I exclaimed, "It was just as good as the last time I had it here."

"Why, you were here before?" Abigail questioned, now gazing at me with a perplexed expression on her face.

"Well, that must have been my last déjà vu experience," I reflexively replied.

"You and your déjà vu, Brian," Abigail quipped, "You know, I do remember the last time I had déjà vu. It was when I called you up to remind you it was our Valentine's Day dinner today at 6:30. And a few days before that, I reminded you it was our Valentine's Day dinner at 6:30 as well. And, as a matter of fact, a few days before *that*, I reminded you it was our Valentine's Day dinner at 6:30. That's my déjà vu experience!"

"I know," I answered apologetically, "I'm sorry. I haven't been in my right mind lately. Maybe I'm studying a little too hard."

After all, I would be correct on that. It's one of the truest things I've said to anyone recently, that I haven't been in my right mind lately.

As Abigail laughed it off, and thanked me for the wonderful dinner, we prepared to leave the restaurant. I would be dropping her off at her house soon. After leaving the restaurant, we approached her house and I walked Abigail to the door, and we said our goodbyes.

After we had said our goodbyes and Abigail closed the door, all was calm and tranquil, and I began to walk off, heading towards the car, when I was, unfortunately, sprayed by a skunk. How could this be? I certainly don't remember this occurrence happening to me. I wonder what changed. I hope everything is gonna be okay between me and Abigail, seeing how the little things change everything sometimes. I'm hoping this doesn't have an impact on our future together. And how am I gonna get this off me now? I'd better head home. Better get washed up. Would rather not head home carrying the skunk scent on me, though. Bad enough I'll smell the car up. Maybe I should jump in a river. Wish I had a bar of soap and some tomato juice. And a dark night too. A very dark night it is. And moonless. A lot of moonless nights. Better head in the car now. I think I have an old blanket in the trunk. Could put it on the seat. That's what I'll do. Put it on the seat.

After placing the blanket on the front seat, I proceeded to enter the car and head back to my dorm. As I began to leave Abigail's house, I remained uncertain as to why, for some mysterious reason, I had been sprayed by this skunk, realizing that never in my life had something of this nature happened. At least I have some tomato juice at my dorm.

Could use that.

As I turned the radio on, I recognized the song that had been playing, only to come to the sudden realization that this song had not been released yet.

"My favorite song," I said to myself.

Fading, getting fainter.

"Yes, my favorite song."

"Yes, my favorite."

Fading, fainter.

"My favorite."

"My favorite."

Fainter.

"Favorite."

Faint.

"My."

Fading.

"Song."

"Song."

"Song."

CHAPTER 34

The Realization

"What's this all about?"

Voices. Voices. Louder. Louder.
"Brian! Brian!"
Sounds. People. Music. Song.
Favorite. Voices. Louder.
"Angela, how is he?"
"He's coming to."
Eyes. Opening. Blurry. Blurred. Focus. Focus,
Brian. Focus. Open your eyes. Open your
eyes and see. See. See.
Hear. Hear. My favorite song. Yes. My
favorite song. You can hear it, Brian. In your
head. Head. You hear it through your head,
Brian. It's all in your head. Coming from

within me.

If I could do it all......over again...
I'd still be with you, I'd still be with you...
If I could do it all......over again...
I'd still be with you...
Just...you...
And only you........................
And only you........................
Hearing. Hearing. Seeing. Seeing Abigail.
Seeing Angela. Standing. Standing over me.
Feeling. Feeling. I feel. I feel as if I am me.
Waking. Waking. Waking into reality.
Coming back. It's all coming back. Back.
Back. I'm back. I'm back! Back! Back! I'm
back! Yes! I'm back!
"I'm back."
I say to myself.
"Brian! You fainted for at least a minute!"
It is Abigail.
"I believe it was vasovagal. He must have
been under heavy stress, and his blood
pressure lowered. He does have low blood
pressure to begin with. I think if he sits
down for a few minutes and has some fluids,
he'll be fine."
It is Angela. Angela. Angela? And how does
she know? And she wanted to be a teacher.
Yes. A teacher.
"Angela," I say as I regain consciousness,

now sitting at a chair nearby, "How do you know it's vasovagal?"

"Brian, I've been a nurse for 20 years now," she says, "I should know vasovagal when I see it. You're a relatively healthy guy, and you've been under a lot of stress preparing for all this. And you do have low blood pressure."

A nurse? Hmm. I guess she did become a nurse.

"Preparing?" I ask, "Preparing for what?"

"Preparing for our 25th anniversary party," Abigail chimes in.

"Oh, that's right, the speech," I say, "Maybe I should make the speech now."

"No, no," Abigail says, "Why don't you rest for a while? You can talk to some people, and then you could make the speech."

"Okay, I guess so," I quietly say.

"Hey, Brian," Rocco says as he approaches me, "Are you okay now?"

"Yeah, yeah, I'm alright now," I say.

"Brian, I want you and Abigail at my restaurant," Rocco exclaims, "Bring the family, it's on the house. I'll never forget the time you put me in my place. You know, at Rocco's Italian Restaurant, I got a five-star rating. I'm well-liked now, and I believe you had something to do with it."

"Oh, well, thank you, Rocco," I respond, "But I must admit, when I did that Ezekiel choke on you, I thought you were gonna pound me. Right now, I don't even think I can do a baby hold, if there even is one."

"Well, don't forget," Rocco reminds me, "Rocco's Italian Restaurant. Bring the family!"

Gee. I guess Rocco done good for himself. Wonder if I had any influence on that. Might have had something to do with it.

"Hey, Rocco," Charles says, "Sally was asking for you. Why don't you go over there and see her?"

"Alright," Rocco replies as he walks off, "And don't forget. Dinner's on me, Brian."

"Well," Charles approaches me, "that was one way to get rid of Rocco. I told him Sally wanted to talk to him. Actually, I wanted to talk to you without being interrupted."

"Come on," I say, "Is that a nice thing to do?"

"Well, hey," Charles says, "that's why I'm a political analyst working for a news agency. Sometimes, you gotta exaggerate the truth. Well, I really don't. I just wanted to talk to you, that's all."

Charles pauses for a moment.

"Did I ever thank you," Charles continues, "for the time you inspired me to join the

Student Council? If it wasn't for that, I probably wouldn't be where I am now."

"Well, I'm glad I was able to help this time around," I reply.

Charles turns as George approaches.

"Oh, hi George," Charles says, "Brian seems to be okay now. Just a little vasovagal."

"What the heck is vasovagal?" George asks Charles, appearing puzzled, "Sounds like a disease."

"Well, let's just say he fainted and he's fine now," Charles concludes, "You can always ask Angela. She'll give you the full details."

"So, Brian," George turns to me, "are you alright now?"

"Oh, I'm fine, George," I say.

"If you want, I can counsel you," George says in a joking tone, "Anything for you, Brian. If it wasn't for you, I'd still be on drugs. Now I counsel people to help them get off drugs."

"Wow, George, that's great," I exclaim, "And your hair looks fantastic! What is that, a crew cut?"

"Yeah, I keep it short now," George says with a chuckle, "It's easier to maintain."

Hmm. I didn't realize I had such an impact on George. Told him to get a haircut, from what I recall. Also told him to stop using pills. And now he's counseling people?

That's a 180°, if I've ever seen one.

As Derek Whitman and my brother Leonard approach me, Charles and George proceed to leave, joining the others, who are seated at their tables.

"Hi Derek," I say as I rise from my seat, "Hi Leonard."

"So, Brian," Leonard says, "Looks like you're back to yourself again."

"Yes, it seems that way," I respond.

"Yeah, you look good, Brian," Derek says.

"What are you guys up to?" I ask, "I saw you both in the corner of the room, talking. You scheming something up or what?"

"Oh, no," Derek replies, "Your brother and I were just talking a little bit about law and order, being he's a lawyer and I'm a police officer."

"Oh, gee," I say, "Now I know where to go in case I need help. I guess crime doesn't pay."

"And I guess stunt work doesn't pay, either," Leonard quips, "'cause that's what I wanted to be once. Didn't work out very well, fortunately. Thanks to my brother, he knows how to subtly encourage you."

"Oh, yes," Derek chimes in, "I did four years in the military, and then became a police officer. And Brian played a big part in me making that decision."

"Well, I'm glad I was able to help," I reply, "Sometimes, all it takes is to be a little bold, and to be there for someone when they really need it."

"Now we could be there for you next time," Derek says, "The next time I see you driving down Somerset Boulevard, exceeding the speed limit, I might just close my eyes."

The three of us laugh and, after laughing, Leonard says, "As for me, I could save you money on your lawyer fees, if Derek decides to arrest you."

"Okay, guys," I respond, "You guys better go back to your corner now."

The two of them say their goodbyes and walk off. As I stand there, looking around, I notice a woman approaching me.

"Brian," the woman says, "I'm so glad you're doing okay now."

"And who may this be?" I ask bewilderedly.

"It's Susan, your sister-in-law," she says, taken aback by my response, "Are you sure you're okay?"

"Oh, yeah, my sister-in-law," I say in surprise, "I was just joking with you. Wanted you to think I was still out of it."

"Well, don't trick me like that," she says, lifting her finger as she walks off, "Trickster."

I can't believe it. Leonard married Susan. The popcorn girl at the movie theater. That's the way to go, Leonard.

As Susan walks off, Jane approaches me with a man. He doesn't look familiar, that's for sure. Maybe it's another one of her boyfriends. Wonder what happened to Alfred. The relationship didn't last, that's for sure.

"Oh, Brian," Jane says, "Glad everything's okay with you now. Roy and I were so worried when we'd seen you hit the floor."

"Yeah, I was really shocked to see that, Brian," Roy says.

Roy? I don't remember a Roy. Could it be? Could it be?

"Roy Harold?" I exclaim abruptly.

"Of course it's me," Roy replies, "Who else do you think it would be?"

"Yes, the one and only Roy," Jane says as she turns to Roy, "My Roy. Brian, I'll never forget the night you encouraged me. If it wasn't for you, Roy and I would most likely not be husband and wife."

"And Brian," Roy says, "if it wasn't for you, I probably wouldn't be here right now. You know what happened after that day I helped you with the photo shoot? It planted a seed in me, and I'm so happy to be a successful news photographer. I've been taking pictures throughout this whole anniversary party of yours, so I'll make sure to send you a professional copy, free of charge."

"That's my Roy," Jane says, "Always doing a good deed."

"Well, I can't thank you enough," I say, "And Jane, you really picked a good one this time." Hmm. Roy and Jane. I never would have thought that in a million years, but I guess anything's possible.

The two of them say their goodbyes and mingle with the party. I then walk off to join Abigail, who is helping serve the desserts. As I approach Abigail, she turns to me, informing me that Sally Hanks will be singing a song while everyone is enjoying dessert. Abigail then tells me that once the song is over, I will be called up to make my speech.

After she informs me of this, I then begin to walk off, leaving the party area. As I leave the party area, I approach the exit door, which leads outside of the church hall.

I step outside to collect my thoughts. I hold my hands over my head, beginning to feel mixed feelings of confusion and astonishment growing over me. Sally Hanks. The last time I remember her singing was at the talent show. And some performance she gave there. And now she's gonna sing at my party. I'd better get back inside. I have to listen to this.

I approached the entrance door, entering the church hall again. As I entered, I began to hear the sound of Sally's voice as she introduced herself to the audience, announcing that she will be touring several cities with her country band. Upon hearing this, the audience applauded her as she turned around to face the DJ, instructing him to play the soundtrack she would sing along to. I wonder if I had anything to do with this, being it seems like I had an effect on so many other people.

As I walked past some of the tables, I noticed Abigail beckoning me over to my table with her hand and, upon noticing this, walked over to my table and sat with Abigail, along with my two daughters, Madison and Mason, who also sat beside me.

The track started to play. Yes. My favorite song. Sally began to sing.

If I could do it all......over again...
I'd still be with you, I'd still be with you...
If I could do it all......over again...
I'd still be with you...
Just...you...

And only you.........................
And only you.........................
She continued to sing for a little while and
the music continued to play, and once the
song had finished, the crowd cheered with
joyous applause.

After a few minutes, I noticed my mother-
in-law gently cradling a baby in her arms.
She then handed the baby to Abigail, and
Abigail, turning to me, handed the baby to
me.

"Abigail," I asked, "What's this all about?"

"Don't you know your own son?" Abigail
said, now giving me strange, uncomfortable
looks.

I was taken aback and in somewhat of a
shock at seeing this. A son? I have a son? The
son that I never had? Boy. I guess I really
made an impact on things. I can't believe it.
I'm holding my own son. Can this get any
better?

"Time for your speech, Brian," Abigail
helpfully reminded me, "and are you sure
you're alright after the fall?"

"I couldn't be any better, Abigail," I replied as
I rose from my seat, handing the baby to
Abigail. If only I knew the baby's name.

CHAPTER 35

The Speech

"I wouldn't change a thing."

The crowd applauded as I approached the stage. I now found myself standing amidst the audience of people, beginning to sense feelings of anxiety and uncertainty coming over me. Now, from what I remember, I had a speech written out. Only it's not in my pocket anymore. Nowhere to be found. I'd better improvise, I guess. Well, here goes.

"First and foremost," I began, now regaining confidence, "I want to start by thanking everyone for being here to celebrate Abigail and my 25th anniversary. It's so great to see everyone, and have this time together with friends and family.

"In our journey through life," I continued, "there are always bumps in the road, and you have to know how to maneuver around those bumps. But sometimes, we can use a helping hand to get around those bumps. And if it weren't for that helping hand, we may end up heading down the wrong road. That's when you may hit more bumps. So if you're ever thinking that you could have done things better in the past, it's never too late to make a change in the present, not only for yourself. But you can help someone make a change in themselves. That, to me, is a wonderful opportunity, and it's an opportunity many people take for granted.

"For example, if I never went for a haircut at *The Cutting Edge*, and if I had never insisted on having Abigail cut my hair, I would not be here celebrating my 25th anniversary with Abigail. Not only do I want to thank Abigail for always being such an encouraging, godly example for our family, but I would also like to thank my two daughters, Madison and Mason, for being the best daughters I could ask for. And as for my son..."

I paused for a moment. If only I knew his name. I'll have to omit that little detail.

"As for my son..." I continued, "I'm excited about the beginnings of this new adventure that is part of our family. I suppose life itself is full of adventures, past, present, and future, and I've experienced all three. But, having thought about it, I've come to the conclusion that, while the journey can certainly be long and arduous, it could also be joyful and worthwhile in the end. And seeing the way everything is now, if I could do it all over again, I wouldn't change a thing."

CHAPTER 36

The Phone Call

"Hey, Brian, I just flew in..."

T he party had come to an end, and we said our goodbyes and thanked everyone for coming. As I was looking for our car in the lot, I couldn't find it, for some strange reason. I asked my wife where the car was, and her response was that I was standing right in front of the car. Upon finding myself standing in front of the car, I noticed that the car was none other than a brand spanking new minivan. I guess we bought it because of our new addition to the family, our son, whatever his name is.

I reached in my pocket and, to my surprise, noticed that I had the keys to the car. I unlocked the car door, and noticed the booster seat in the backseat for our son. Madison and Mason began to strap our son into the booster seat.

"This car smells showroom fresh," I remarked to Abigail as we entered the car. "Well, what do you want?" Abigail replied, "We picked it up last week from the dealer." Gee. I didn't think I could afford a car like this. Then again, anything's possible. Boy, what a ride this is. And so smooth. Wonder what the gas mileage is.

"Dad," Madison said, "Why don't you sing the song you always sing to Michael? It helps put him to sleep."

Oh boy. I guess that's his name. My son's name. Michael. At least that helps. Only I don't know what the song is. I have an idea. I have an idea.

"Madison, why don't you start off?" I requested.

She started off the song and, thankfully, I knew the lyrics, and followed her lead.

As we pulled into our driveway, I realized that we are still living in the same house. At least that didn't change. I kinda like this house.

We entered the door and, upon entering, I found myself jumped on by what looked to be a Labradoodle.

"Down, Teddy!" Abigail called out, "Mason, let the dog out in the back."

Mason led the dog toward the door that led to the outdoors, and opened it. Hmm. A Labradoodle. Named Teddy? I wonder who picked out that name.

"And Madison," Abigail said, "Could you feed Pokey?"

Pokey? What do we got, another dog? Maybe a cat.

"Here, Pokey! Here, Pokey!" I called out.

"Dad," Madison said, "Pokey's in his turtle tank. Why would you call for Pokey?"

"Oh, just messing around," I replied in quiet embarrassment.

"I don't know," Madison said, "Ever since he fainted, Mom, he's been acting strange. Are you sure it was the vasovagal that did it?"

"Well, as forgetful as he is," Abigail replied, "let's see if he forgets to eat his snack before he goes to bed tonight. If he eats his snack, then we can conclude that he's normal."

"Well," Madison said, "even if he doesn't forget his snack, I doubt that he'll ever be completely normal."

"I heard that, Madison!" I exclaimed.

After a couple minutes of talking with Abigail and the girls, I proceeded to eat a couple leftover cannolis from the party. After I finished my brief snack, I headed upstairs and, upon entering the bedroom, noticed a new message on our answering machine.

I pressed the play button, and to my surprise, the voice speaking on the voice message was that of Harry Ferguson. He said:

"Hey, Brian, I just flew in from overseas. My 30-year stint in the military has expired, and I knew I had to talk to you. You'd be the first one I'd have to contact. It's been a while since we've talked. Call me back. I'd like to talk to you. I know it's probably going to be late when you get this, but call me, no matter what time. Goodbye."

The message ended. Harry. Harry Ferguson. I can't believe it's him. I haven't heard from him in a long time. It's best I call him now and see how he's doing.

I called up Harry and asked how he was doing. He told me a little bit about how he's been, but then said that he wanted to save the rest of the details for when we get together, and being it's late, he didn't want to keep me up. I suggested that we have breakfast at Palmer's Diner tomorrow morning at 8pm, before church.

After several minutes, Abigail entered the bedroom. I looked up to find her standing near the door.

"Who were you on the phone with at this hour?" Abigail asked.

"Can you believe that Harry Ferguson just left me a voice message?" I replied, "I returned his phone call, and tomorrow, we're gonna have breakfast at Palmer's Diner."

"Do you know, there's church tomorrow?" Abigail said.

"Yeah, but church starts at 10:30," I answered, "we agreed to meet at 8:00."

"Okay," Abigail agreed, "Tomorrow, we're having our baby dedication service for Michael."

Boy, I really need some updates on what's going on here. I could use some updates. Everywhere I turn, something seems to be different. Perhaps I've crossed a fabric of time. Probably. But at least I have my mind together. And there's one thing I do know. I have my appetite. Those cannolis I had were really good, so at least I've got it together in that sense.

CHAPTER 37

The Final Chapter

(Or is it?)

"What happened to me?"

As I pulled into the parking lot of Palmer's Diner, I noticed Harry Ferguson walking out of his car. Boy, he hasn't changed one bit in 30 years. I got out of my car, and approached Harry as he headed towards the entrance door to the diner. We greeted each other with a handshake and a hug, and then headed into the diner.

As we were brought to our seats, I asked Harry if he would be ordering the usual. Harry responded with "Of course", and that the last time he had it at this diner was 30 years ago. I then briefly looked at one of the menus on our table, but we had already decided on what we wanted to order beforehand.

As we were eating our breakfast, me having my buttermilk pancakes with bacon on the side, Harry having his chocolate-chip pancakes with sausage on the side, Harry had been telling me about when he started his 30-year military stint right after high-school graduation.

After 20 minutes or so of Harry explaining to me about his time in the military overseas, I began to think about how I was going to explain to Harry the situation I found myself experiencing since I fainted. Nonetheless, I waited for Harry to finish his story about his time in the military.

"Harry," I said in surprise, "You really got to travel a lot in the military. All those different countries you got to see. And you learned three other languages? And a wife and three kids that traveled around with you on different military bases?"

"Exactly," Harry confirmed, "And, you know

what? I even learned a little bit of the Chamorro language when I was stationed in Guam. I only really know a couple words and phrases though, but just basic conversation. The only languages I'd say I'm really fluent in, though, are German, Italian, and Japanese."

"I'm still learning English myself," I said, "being my daughters use so many slang terms, I don't know what they're saying half of the time."

We both laughed at this before the waitress approached us and asked how our food was.

"Excellent, just as it was 30 years ago," I replied, and the waitress smiled for a moment before she walked off to attend to another table.

"Well, I'm excited to hear how you're doing, Brian," Harry said.

"Harry," I began with uncertainty, "You're the only person I can trust, so I probably should tell you what's really been going on with me. The story I'm about to tell you, in my mind, is all true, and really happened. And I honestly, undoubtedly feel, that this experience I went through was as real and vivid as this conversation."

"I'm all ears, Brian," Harry replied.

I began telling the story of all that had

happened, starting from the morning of my 25th anniversary, then taking Harry through the series of events that unfolded during my brief fainting episode at the party, and concluded at the end of that night.

"That's a really neat story," Harry said, "Really amazing if true. Not that I don't believe you. It's just a story that is somewhat hard to believe. But being I've been in the military for 30 years, I could believe just about anything."

"Well, that's why I wanted to tell you," I replied, "'cause I knew you'd understand."

"But Brian," Harry said, "you never mentioned what happened to me. You mentioned what happened to Roy, Jane, Derek, and the others, but you never mentioned what happened to me. What happened to me?"

"Well," I paused for a few seconds, lowering my head in pensive sadness, "I wasn't planning on telling you. Are you sure you want me to continue?"

"I guess the story wouldn't be complete if you left me out," Harry responded.

"Well," I began somberly, "it was the night of the high-school graduation party. You were hardly sober. You had drunk a little too much that night. You drove home that night, but you never made it home."

There was an unsettling silence for several seconds, and we sat there for a moment, silently contemplating the words, the words and their mysteriously unsettling tone.

"But what happened?" Harry asked in a confused tone.

"That was the night you were killed in an automobile accident, Harry," I replied, then followed this reply with a sad, reflective sigh.

"But…" Harry paused, "how do you explain me being here? I'm alive, I'm not some ghost."

"Because in the past," I began, "at the end of the party, as you were heading toward the car, I took the keys from you, so you couldn't drive home. And that's why you're here today."

"Well, Brian," Harry said, "I guess I can't thank you enough. How could I ever repay you?"

"Well," I replied with a grin, "you can buy breakfast."

Alternate Ending

"Wondering what happened last night, or will happen tonight…"

The Saturday morning.

BRIAN exits the bedroom, heading toward the kitchen.

ABIGAIL
Hey, Mason, let's go!

MASON refrains from leaving her bedroom.

MADISON
Gee, how many times are you gonna call her, Mom?

ABIGAIL
Oh, well, she'll just have to deal with cold
pancakes.

BRIAN enters the kitchen.

BRIAN
[entering]
Well, that's what happens when you're in a
house full of women.

BRIAN opens the refrigerator door to grab the
orange juice.

MADISON
Hey, Dad! I'm never late.

BRIAN
Well, maybe you were supposed to be the boy we
never had.

And BRIAN is still wondering what happened
last night, or will happen tonight at the 25th
anniversary party.

Author's Epilogue

First and foremost, I would like to say that I hope you enjoyed this book and had a fun time reading it.

But let me guess. You're confused and you want some clarification. You may be thinking this: it was all a dream. You may also be thinking this: it's all a continuous time loop. You may also be thinking this: it all really happened and ended in the final chapter. Whether Brian was experiencing a dream, a time loop, or a reality, I cannot clarify.

But for a moment, put yourself in Brian's place. Brian felt he could have changed people's lives for the better and that he didn't contribute enough to the future. Whether he actually changed things or not, it's up to you to decide. But have you ever thought sometimes that maybe you could've done something to change things or people for the better?

I don't believe we can change the past. I think the only change we can make is to change the present. Either way, you can change the present which will affect the future. That is what I believe. Don't look back at the past, and what you could have changed. It's not worth it.

The present is all you need to focus on now, and the future is something you can look forward to. I just want you to know that I would like for you to close this book knowing one thing. You may not be able to do things all over again, as Brian did (or maybe he didn't), but there's one thing that you can do. And there's still time: to start all over again.

God bless you.

Paul & Luke Conzo

About The Authors

Paul & Luke Conzo are a father-and-son writing team, All Over Again being their first novel. Paul is a retired mechanic, machinist, landscaper, tile installer, and helpdesk technician—a jack of all trades, in other words. Luke is an A-student and a talented writer and musician. Paul and Luke like to write science-fiction, fantasy, and dramas with a twist. Luke participated in a literary competition among the schools of Stamford, and was awarded the first-place prize for his poem, in the category of 11th and 12th Grade Nonfiction. Paul and Luke reside in Norwalk, Connecticut.

Made in United States
North Haven, CT
16 June 2024

53453475R00137